Puffin Books . Editor: Kaye Webb

VIKING'S SUNSET

The idea of Harald Sigurdson's last voyage came to
Henry Treece when a young friend of his told him of
the finding of the prow of a Viking longship in a lake in
North America. He set out to devise a story round the
kind of man who could make this incredible voyage
from Scandinavia to the then unknown continent.

This book is the story of how Harald and his friend
Giant Grummoch from *The Road to Miklagard*, set out
in pursuit of marauding Vikings who have raided their
homesteads, but instead of catching Haakon Redeye and
his vicious companions, are swept by rough seas to
far-off Greenland. Here they are befriended by Eskimos,
and then sail still further westwards, to the land of the
redskins, where Harald meets warriors as proud as his
own, and fights against treachery crueller than death
itself.

In this final, moving volume of Henry Treece's trilogy
of the Vikings, there is a shatteringly vivid picture of the
stark fate of these early seafarers, and of the brave
spirit with which they rose to meet it.

Cover design by Victor Ambrus

D1080951

Viking's Sunset

Henry Treece

Illustrated by Christine Price

Puffin Books in association with The Bodley Head

Puffin Books, Penguin Books Ltd,
Harmondsworth, Middlesex, England
Penguin Books Australia Ltd, Ringwood,
Victoria, Australia
Penguin Books Canada Ltd,
41 Steelcase Road West,
Markham, Ontario, Canada
Penguin Books (N. Z.) Ltd,
182–190 Wairau Road,
Auckland 10, New Zealand

First published by The Bodley Head 1960
Published in Puffin Books 1967
Reprinted 1971, 1974, 1975
Copyright © the Estate of Henry Treece, 1960

Made and printed in Great Britain by
C. Nicholls & Company Ltd
Set in Linotype Juliana

For Gary Faysash –
who told me of the longship prow

Contents

About this Book

This is the third and last book about Harald Sigurdson. In VIKING'S DAWN, he was a lad of fifteen, voyaging in the longship *Nameless* to the Hebrides; in THE ROAD TO MIKLAGARD, he and the giant Grummoch made the long journey down to Constantinople to join the Palace Guard there. Now, in VIKING'S SUNSET, Harald is a mature man and the date is A.D. 815.

In this book he is a prosperous farmer, with a family of his own, who sails out from Norway on a voyage of revenge and, almost by accident, reaches Iceland and later the southern tip of Greenland, before setting off again, in *Long Snake*, to even stranger places. . . .

Here I should halt a moment to say that recorded history tells us that Iceland was discovered by one Naddodd in A.D. 867, and Greenland in A.D. 985, by Eric Röde who was flying from Norway to escape a charge of manslaughter.

But I have a theory that recorded history, especially of the early voyages, often lags behind *actual* history. For instance, we don't really know when the early Mediterranean travellers first 'discovered' Britain – though recorded history tells us that the Greek astronomer Pytheas came here in the fourth century B.C. I would guess that a cautious scholar like Pytheas would have a pretty good idea, from *unrecorded* travellers' yarns, what he was going to find !

And so I feel justified in letting Harald Sigurdson

anticipate Naddodd by a mere fifty-two years. After all, the longships of Harald's time were superb creations, quite capable of the voyages I describe; and the questing spirit of the Northmen was as lively in A.D. 815 as it was in A.D. 867.

In my other books I have tried to describe what vikings were like, but to explain VIKING'S SUNSET I must add a little more. The Northmen were immensely brave and hardy; they were also savage and superstitious. They were still pagans when the rest of Europe had long become Christianised. In some ways they were like children – very dangerous children ! To the Franks, English and Irish, they seemed like devils, and prayers were offered up in the churches as a protection against them. On the other hand, when the odds were in favour of the English, they treated these Northmen ruthlessly, even flaying them and nailing their skins on church doors, or flinging the ambushed marauders into adder-pits. There were no doubt faults on both sides, for in history no one is ever completely in the right.

What attracts me most about the Northmen is their story-telling. From the Sagas we learn of many fantastic people and their incredible adventures, all told with the great craft and gusto of the Skald. Sometimes, these tales are full of repetition – as children's fairy-tales often are – and sometimes they are told so laconically, so briefly, that we almost have to guess what really happened ! But almost always they are told with a dry and even a grim sense of humour, for the men of the North were not given to self-pity. They joked even in the face of death; which, after all, was to them only the beginning of a new life in Valhalla, the 'Slaughter Hall'.

In this book I have made an attempt to use the viking style of story-telling, whenever it seemed right. I have also tried to show what a *berserk* was like, for I think that we must consider these strange creatures if we are to understand many of the things our curious forefathers did.

The bullfighter, dressing-up to go into the arena; the boxer, chatting with his seconds before a fight; the racing-driver, laughing at a funny story in the 'pits' before the flag goes down, are all brave men: but they are taking a calculated risk, which they assume will bring them money – the more the better!

The *berserk*, stamping himself into a fury, biting his shield-rim, bellowing in the cold air without a stitch on him, had no fortune to gain by his actions. If he saw anything awaiting him at all, it was a grimly-held wall of spear-points, just fifty yards away....

Undoubtedly, the berserk was crazy; but, as Alan Breck said to Davy Balfour in *Kidnapped*, 'Och, man, but am I no a bonny fechter!' And who can help liking a bonny fechter, however crazy he may be?

One more point: in Minnesota there was discovered a stone inscribed with viking symbols. This fact struck no chord in my mind until one day an American boy who comes to see me said, 'Didn't you know, some of our archaeologists have found the prow of a longship in one of the lakes?'

Then I did know – not in the historian's way, but in the story-teller's way – just what happened to Harald Sigurdson and his shipload of vikings!

What I 'know' I am telling you in this book; but what Harald Sigurdson found out, he told to no man, for reasons which you will discover. HENRY TREECE

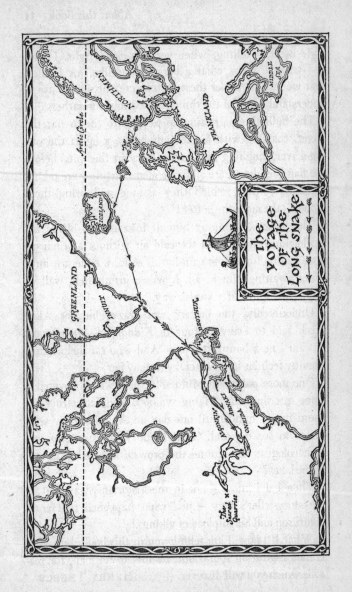

The Voyage of the Long Snake

Chapter **I** *The Barn-Burners*

It was Spring. Harald Sigurdson and Giant Grummoch were tending a sick cow up above Jagsfjord, with the wind blowing them half off their feet, when a shock-headed thrall came running up the hill to them.

Grummoch heard him and said, 'That is Jango No-breeches. When he runs the world's end is near, for he is the laziest thrall between here and Miklagard.'

Jango called out to them, long before he reached them, 'Come quickly, masters !'

Harald said, 'If the meat is burning, turn the spit and roast the other side. This cow is in calf and it would ill become me to leave her because the meat was burning.'

The thrall began to wring his hands. The wind carried away his words the first time. Then they heard him say, 'The meat is burning with a vengeance, master. But it would ill become me to meddle with it.'

Harald Sigurdson had grown into a stern man, with grey wolf's hair, in the twenty years he had been head-man of his village, after the death of Thorn. Now few men dared stand against him in his anger, save Jomsvik-ings or Russians from Kiev, and they did not come up the hill every day.

But the thrall would not be silent. He ran to Harald and even took him by the sleeve of his leather jacket, which was a thing few men would have done save Giant Grummoch, who was his blood-brother and the second father to Harald's two sons, Svend and Jaroslav.

The thrall said, 'A wise man would come, even if twenty cows lay on the turf in calf, Harald Sigurdson. You have three barns a-burning, and your wife, Asa Thornsdaughter, leaving her broken spinning-wheel in bitter tears over the wounds of your two sons.'

Harald turned to him now and said, 'I shall whip you for stealing the barley beer we had laid by for the Spring feasting, Jango No-breeches. You have fallen asleep and dreamed a dream. You listen too much to the skalds about the night-fires. Go back and dip your head in a bucket of water.'

The thrall flung himself onto the turf and began to roll about, wailing, for he was of the Irish folk and given to such demonstrations. Grummoch picked him up with one hand and held him out before him like a girl's rag doll, with his two legs dangling.

'Say your message, if there is one, then go home like a good dog,' he said gruffly, his beard wagging close to the frightened thrall's face.

Jango No-breeches said, 'By Saint Colmkill and the Whitechrist, Haakon Redeye has been here while you were away. What torch has not done, axe has achieved. Down there is no more village left than a man could stow in a longship and carry away – and all charred timber.'

Giant Grummoch put the man down.

The thrall said, 'I bring black news, not white, master. Many have gone to Odin in the last hour. Many have made the long dark journey and hang by their necks from the trees. Haakon Redeye brought eighty berserks with him, and only the young folk and the old were left in the village. How could they stand against eighty berserks with war axes and spears? Your sons were hurt with the others.'

Harald said, 'I do not ask if they are badly hurt, or near to death. I only ask if they carry their wounds on their chests.'

The thrall nodded. 'Aye, master,' he said. 'On their chests and their arms and their heads – but not on their backs.'

Grummoch, who loved the two boys, took up a piece of black bog-oak as thick as a man's lower leg, and broke it across his thigh to show his rage.

'In all the Northland,' he said, 'there is only one man who would do such things to old folk and young folk, and that man shall feel his neck snap like this twig before the day is over.'

The thrall said, 'Haakon Redeye has already sailed, master Giant. You must needs mount a swan and fly after him if you would catch him. But let us go down, and save what we can of the village. I am but a simple man and no warrior, but I counsel thus.'

Harald said, 'I am forty years old and looked to sit back in peace in my age. I thought my voyaging was over when I came from Miklagard, but now it seems I must put an edge on my sword again, if I can still lift it.'

The thrall looked at Harald's big muscles and his broad back, but did not speak, for he had learned not to interrupt warriors and shieldmen when they began their boasting.

Harald said, 'By this cow and her calf, I swear that I will harry Haakon Redeye to the edge of the world and will at last set his polished head on my shelf to smile at before this tale is over, for what he has done to me.'

Grummoch, who had picked up the manners of the Northmen in his years beside the fjord, said, 'When I have visited his berserks, they will ask each other why the thunder was so loud, and why the lightning came so suddenly. That is, if they still have heads to ask with.'

Jango No-breeches said, 'Come, come, masters. There will be time to bite the shield-rim and to bellow later, when you have seen what work is to be avenged.'

Then he ran on along the slippery path towards the village and the others followed him, feeling it no shame to be led by a thrall, this time.

Chapter 2 *The Sailing*

It was as bad as the thrall had said. Out of thirty-seven houses, only six remained, and no barns.

Harald looked at the old ones and the young ones who lay, no longer fearsome of the axe, and said, 'To call this a bad business is to blow out hot air from the mouth. The only word is in the sword from this day forward. Where is my family?'

The thrall led him to where Asa Thornsdaughter sat, weeping and rocking back and forth. Her two sons lay on a pallet of straw, their wounds covered with moss. Harald lifted the moss before he spoke to her and then said, 'My boys have fought like warriors. Their wounds will heal, Odin be praised, for they are cleanly dressed.'

Asa said through her tears, 'Boys of ten and twelve should not be asked to carry wounds so early on, husband.'

Harald said, 'Asa, loved one, do you expect me to weep like a woman or a thrall when my sons are hurt? The old bear does not love to see his cubs mauled by the wolf – but he knows there is no profit in sitting howling. He knows that for a finger he must take an arm; for a hand, a head. The old bear will go after the wolf and seek his bargain, for Haakon Redeye is outlaw and wolf's-head and will not stand before the Thing to receive sentence. He will not pay the blood-money, so he must pay with his head.'

Asa began to cry again, and put her apron over her face so that no one should see the wife of a viking weeping.

And when the other young men came back to the village, Harald met them and said, 'There has been a slight mishap while you were away in the woods catching hares. The village has been burned down through an oversight of Haakon Redeye, and your families have been entertained by eighty of his berserks. It seems that he was so upset by the nuisance his visit has caused that he has gone away to hang his head in shame.'

A young axe-warrior, given to fits when he was excited, stepped forward and ripped off his own shirt. His chest was covered with scars and so were his arms, from wrist to elbow.

He shook a great axe in his right hand as though it were a little elder stick. 'Before Thor and Odin,' he said, 'I will not rest until I have shamed Haakon's head still further.'

Harald said, 'There you make a mistake, my friend. Haakon's head is not yours for the shaming. I have laid claim to that prize already.'

The young berserk bowed his head, but whispered to his nearest friend that Harald must take his chance when they ran up alongside Haakon Redeye, for in a case like this all men had equal rights, headman or henchmen.

Then they drew out the longship from the creek where it was hidden under bracken and gorse, and they examined its timbers to see if it needed tarring again.

Gudbrod Gudbrodsson said, 'This steerboard side needs caulking, Harald Sigurdson, but there is no time to waste, and we have helmets to bale out the water. They will do as well as any buckets !'

Harald said, 'I will stick my finger in the hole if it comes to it, Gudbrod Gudbrodsson. Throw aboard dried meat, barley bread and two casks of ale, and then we will be off. A man must eat if he is to pay his debts with sword and axe.'

Before he left, he kissed Asa most tenderly and told her that he was leaving twenty men behind to guard them and to set up shelters for them once more.

He told her also that he expected to be back in three days, for his sixty shipmen were capable of repaying all the debts they owed to Haakon Redeye and his eighty.

'A man with vengeance in his sword-edge is the equal of four who have burned a barn,' he said, buckling on his iron friend, *Peace-giver*.

Asa said, 'Have you got your woollen shirt on, husband? The Spring winds are bitter along the fjords and it would go ill with a war leader to be stricken with a cold.'

Harald said, 'I shall keep warm with exercise soon, my love.'

When he bent over the bed of his two sons, Svend and Jaroslav, the boys smiled up at him and said, 'May Odin speed the prow, father.'

Harald said, 'I am blessed in having a pair of young hawks when many other fathers have only chickens.'

Svend said, 'If we could stand up, we would come with you, whether you agreed or not.'

Jaroslav said, 'I shall weep all the time you are gone, for I put a knife into Haakon's arm before he struck me down with his club. It is not fair that I cannot finish what I have started.'

Harald patted their heads and said, 'Rest awhile, my

pretties, then one day you shall have long swords and go after such pirates as Redeye yourselves, while I lie in the straw and think of my cows and the ships I have sailed in.'

Svend said, 'Bring me back Haakon's dagger with the coral handle. And bring back his bronze shield for Jaroslav. It will help us to get better more quickly.'

As Harald went down to the longship, Asa whispered, 'Bring me back something we can put on the shelf and smile at in the feasting times, loved one. Something closer to Haakon Redeye even than his knife and his shield.'

Harald said, 'If I do not do that, I shall do nothing. An ornament is always pleasant in a house, Asa Thornsdaughter. But if the dice fall otherwise than what I think, then get yourself a cross of the Whitechrist and set that up as your ornament to smile at, for then you will know that Thor and Odin are no longer our friends.'

Asa did not watch as they pushed out into the fjord. She hated to see the longships sail away, for sometimes they never came back, and then there was always the misery of remembering how fine they had looked when they set off, with the gay oars rising and falling in unison, and the shipmaster laughing at the prow.

Chapter 3 *Cold Scent*

The days passed as Harald's ship, *Long Snake*, drew in and out of the fjords seeking Haakon Redeye, and each day brought wild-haired villagers running down to the shore, shaking their heads, saying that Haakon had not stayed there, but had passed on north, and north again.

One grey-headed jarl waded into the green waters of Langfjord and shouted, 'They passed this way a day since, the wind in their red and blue sails, ship laden to waterline with plunder. You must needs row harder, Harald Sigurdson, to catch that wolf by the tail. I doubt you'll not find him in Norway. He'll be gone to the far north, to Isafjord Deep, or to Vatnsfjord. He'll be gone to where the white fox runs and the walrus snorts, mark my word.'

So *Long Snake* turned about once more, and headed northwards.

Harald stood by Grummoch, near the steer-boardman.

'I swear by the fingers of two hands that I will not give up this chase until Haakon or I lie stark,' he said.

Grummoch said, 'There is not a man aboard who will not sail with you to Iceland, or to Midgard itself, Harald. Ask them and see.'

Then Harald spoke to the vikings.

'Who will turn back?' he said. 'Who will go back to eat fresh meat and lie snug under the blankets? Let any such man speak now and I will set him ashore with an axe in his hand and money in his pouch to make his way back to the village. Speak now or forever hold your peace.'

Then the seamen turned towards Harald and shook their axes above their heads.

'Who goes back now is a *nithing*,' one called out. 'Do you wish to insult us, Sigurdson?'

Harald answered, 'Thorfinn Thorfinnson, I would as soon insult your namesake, Thor, himself. From now on, I shall ask that question no more. Let us sail onwards, and whosoever comes alive out of this quest, let the skalds name him a hero of the folk.'

Then Thorfinn Thorfinnson began to beat with a hammer on the floorboard to set the rowing-time, and all backs bent to the oars. And as they rowed, Thorfinn sang an old song which they all knew:

> 'Makers of widows, wander we must;
> Killers 'tween seedtime and salting of kine;
> Walking the Whale's Way, sailing the Swan's Path,
> Daring the Sun's Track, tricking dark death!
> In jaws of the storm, jesting we stand,
> Lashed with hail's fury, hand frozen to line;
> Numb head rain-shaken, sharp spume in the nostril,
> Salt caking hair – and blood's haven in sight!'

All the men joined in, feeling once more the sharp splash of the water on their faces, breathing deep of the salt-laden air after the long winter ashore.

And many that day blessed Haakon Redeye for giving them the excuse to sail again and to leave the barley field and the pig-sty.

Late that night, on a little skerry of stones that hardly poked above the sea's level, they heard a man crying out to them. As they drew nearer the voice, they saw that big white sea birds circled over the rocks, as though to threaten the man who clung there so desperately.

As they came alongside, they saw a man dressed in an old horsehide clinging to the stones, too weak to draw himself up away from the sea's hands.

Harald called out, 'What man are you?'

And the man answered weakly, 'I am Havlock Ingolfson, master. Haakon Redeye had me flung into the sea because I wanted my share of the plunder now and not when we reached Isafjord Deep. Save me, I beg you.'

Harald said, 'Were you with the men who burned Sigurdson's Steading three days ago?'

The man said, 'Aye, master, and a fine burning we made of it. Take me aboard and I will tell you the story. It will make you smile, I warrant you.'

Then Harald took his axe in his hand and for a while

seemed about to leap into the water and put an end to this rogue. But at last he turned away and said to the rowers, 'Why should I hurry his end? Let the Dark Ones who weave our web have their way with him. Set course to northwards again, my seacocks!'

So *Long Snake* passed on, and soon the wretch began to yell out again as the sea birds came back and swirled over him in the dusk.

And at last the men on *Long Snake* heard him crying out no more.

That night they lay out in open sea, three leagues off land, with the top-cover down over the roof-slats, and their sheep-skins about them.

And as Harald paced the deck, unable to sleep for the thought of his revenge, he thought the mists before the longship parted and a woman wearing a winged helmet and carrying a shield stood upon the prow looking down at him, smiling strangely.

Harald said, 'What have you come to tell me, Shield-maiden? Speak out in clear words for I am afraid of nothing now.'

Then the Shield-maiden spoke and her voice was like the splintering of icicles and sometimes like the swishing that the gannet makes as he falls out of the cold sky.

She said, 'Harald Sigurdson, I have come to bring no message, but only to look on your face, so that I shall know you again.'

Then Harald said, 'Why should you need to know me, Shield-maiden? Are you to bring my doom upon me?'

Then the grey misty shape seemed to laugh, with a sound like the grey seals mourning on some lonely skerry out beyond Iceland.

And at last she said, 'We do not answer the questions of men. We do the bidding of the gods only.'

Harald Sigurdson said, 'Many a time have I heard of you doomsters, yet never have I seen you before, though I have lain helpless in the deep sea off the Western Isles with my body numb and my mind gone from me.'

The woman said, 'We come but once, to be seen by men. And when we come the second time, they do not see us.'

Then Harald said, 'I understand, Shield-maiden. I see that I have done something wrong. I will not ask you what it was, for I think I know now. I should not have left that wretch on the skerry for the seas to drown and the birds to eat.'

Then the Shield-maiden seemed to nod her head and whispered, 'When the winds howl over the lonely nesses and the snow beats across the frozen inlets, you will remember him, remember Havlock Ingolfson, who lived wrong but died right.'

Harald said, 'I will turn the ship round to find him, Shield-maiden.'

But she only laughed and whispered, 'Too late. Too late . . .'

And then, as Harald went forward to see her more clearly, she faded back from the tall prow and into the rocking sea.

So Harald shrugged his shoulders and then went back to the stern shelter and wrapped his blanket about him and fell into a numbed sleep, which lasted him until the dawn.

Chapter 4 *Distant Waters*

The next morning broke clear and cold as crystal. A flurry of kittiwakes swept about the longship; then three stormy petrels came so low that their wings almost touched the mast. A dark cloud built up like a grey fortress on the port quarter, and then a grim wind started up, whipping the salt spume across men's backs as they rowed, as sharp as a whiplash.

Grummoch, who was half as big again as any Northman, got the full force of this, down to the waist, and so ruefully lay down under the lee of the shield-gunwale.

It was as he lay thus that Harald went to him and said, 'Shame would it be on me, not to tell my oath-brother and the foster-father of my children what I have seen in the night.'

Grummoch said, 'This day will test us all. There are berserks here who will weep for a cup of warm milk and a sizzling hunk of pork, before this day is out. What did you see, brother?'

Harald told him of the Shield-maiden and of what she had said.

Then Grummoch raised himself on his big red elbow and said, 'All men must go when the Norns call. Yet I have it in my mind that your dream was more the result of too little food and too much excitement yesterday. I think you will live to be a hundred.'

Harald almost struck his oath-brother then for so

tempting the gods; but instead he held down his hand and said after a while, 'The guest who stays longest at the feast sees the most juggling.'

Then he went aft to tell the man at the steerboard to lash his helm to the ship-side, so that they might hold their course to the north.

An hour later the full force of the Spring storm hit them, rocking *Long Snake* as though she were a ship of straw. Few men that day ate; and those that ate scantly kept down their meals. And so it was for three more days and nights, until the men of the longship began to swear that Haakon Redeye was in league with Loki the Wicked, or that Freya, the Goddess, who saw to the bringing forth of life, had turned her back on them and intended them to feed the fishes, and so help bring forth fish-life.

But Harald laughed at them, and did not tell them of his vision of the Shield-maiden. Instead, he told them not to be thrallish-minded, and said that he had sailed through storms ten times worse than this one when he was a young man; though he knew that he lied.

*

At last, when the long low shape of the land of ice raised itself up over the black sea, most men in *Long Snake* lay on the boards, groaning and asking their friends to slip a knife below their ribs so that they might not have to endure another day of this torment. Wet to the bone, raw at elbow and knee, their stomachs empty of food, these men had hardly the strength to lift sword or axe now.

Harald said to Grummoch, 'These men are in poor case. Not one, save thee and me, could swing a sword or flail an axe.'

Grummoch said, 'Count me out. If a kitten leapt at my throat, I could not save myself. I should be at its mercy!'

Harald smiled to think of the kitten who could spring high enough to reach tall Grummoch's throat, but he said nothing and went forward to where Gudbrod Gudbrodsson lay, making little marks on the planks with his wet finger.

'Friend,' said the shipmaster, 'you know of the inlets and nesses of this place. Where are we to steer?'

Gudbrod Gudbrodsson said without looking up, 'I have heard of these places from my grandfather, who sailed here in a storm when he had not enough money to pay for the killing of Alkai Nobody. But when he told me, he was in his dotage and rambled. I cannot remember what the old sheep said, master. All I know is that he said the place was full of lawless men who had come here to avoid hanging or head-removing. That is all I know.'

Then he went on scribbling over the decks, using his finger as pen, and salt-water as ink, daft with the storm and hunger.

Harald went to the steerboard and unlashed it. Then he scanned the coastline that stretched out before him.

As a cloud of birds came out to meet *Long Snake*, Harald put the helm hard over, towards a place under a hill, where a cloud of dark brown smoke rose.

The longship lay in a sheltered waterway, full of shoals, that afternoon. The vikings waded ashore, each trying to look fierce, but each cursing the day when Haakon Redeye fetched them out on this blood-quest.

There was a half-rotting whale drawn up on the shore and many men about it, hacking for blubber with great adzes and flensing-knives. They had a huge fire of seaweed beside them, on which iron pots bubbled as they flung the blubber pieces into them. The stench was heavy. Even the birds avoided that place.

Harald went foremost, with Grummoch close behind him.

The men flensing the whale scantly looked up. They were red-eyed fellows, wearing old clothes and their feet bound with sheep-skins. Their hair and beards flapped matted and uncombed in the shore wind. Not one carried a true weapon, but only staves tipped with iron.

As the vikings approached, a short bandy-legged man rose from his business of lifting out the whale's heart and came, red-handed, a pace or two to meet them. His face was set and defiant.

Harald said in Norse, 'Greetings, friend. We seek Haakon Redeye. Can you tell us where he may be?'

The man looked up at the sky. Then he looked to left and to right. Then he spat into the scummy water of the shore puddles.

'He is not here,' he said. 'He is not at Isafjord Deep. Maybe at Ragnafjord, or at Sealflaying fjord. I do not know, and I care less. But not here.'

He spoke in a strange dialect that Harald could hardly understand, as though he had always lived at this place and had learned from seals and walruses and the gulls rather than from men. Harald did not like the looks of him, for his eyes were dark and set close together. Besides, his eyebrows were so sandy-light that who could see them unless he came very close, too close?

All the time he spoke, his score or so of men stood silent about the rotting whale, their adzes in their raw hands, their chapped lips closed, their matted hair blowing in the wind.

Grummoch went forward and said slowly, 'If I took you by the leg, I could fling you over that hill.'

The man said, 'What good would that do you or me? It would not tell you what you want to know, and it would stop me from flensing my whale. Don't talk like a fool. Your body has outgrown your brain.'

Harald said, 'I would give good pieces of money to know where Haakon Redeye is at this moment.'

The man said, 'There are no markets here. No place to use money, friend. We have horses and pigs and sheep. We have fish and whale-blubber. What use is money to us?'

Harald saw that they could neither frighten nor buy this man.

He said, 'Suppose we burn your village down, what then? What would your wives say to that?'

The man said, 'They know better than to raise their voices. They are all lawless women who have sailed with pirates years ago. They have burned villages themselves, and they have built villages. Besides, they never speak unless we give them leave. They are well-trained, unlike the women of Norway and Denmark. If you burn our village, you are welcome to do so. And while you do that, we shall stave in the sides of your longship with our flensing adzes. That is all.'

Grummoch said, 'Suppose we kill you all, here and now?'

The man said, 'If I blow this bone whistle on my belt, fifty more men will come running from behind that hill, and fifty more from the next one. Then they will do such things to you that I have not the words to speak of.

Go away and waste no more of our time with your prattle.'

The man then turned back to the whale, and his fellows bent again to their stinking task.

Harald said to Grummoch, 'This fellow is lying. He knows more than he will say – yet his reasoning is good. There is nothing we can do to make him tell us where Haakon Redeye might be.'

Grummoch said, 'It ill becomes warriors to turn back from such a creature. But there is little we can do. Let us go back to the ship.'

As they went, the men about the whale scoffed at them in their hoarse voices, and flung pieces of bone and skin after them. But the vikings did not turn back, though sometimes they were sorely tempted, especially when the rubbish struck them.

Long Snake set forth again, and rounded the headland and so came into deeper waters, where the grey rock rose high on either side of them. And as they went, they saw fires start up here and there on the hillsides, as though signals were being sent from one part of the place to another.

Thorfinn Thorfinnson said, 'Seems it to me that who catches Redeye must have windows in the back of his head.'

Gudbrod Gudbrodsson said, 'And a sword in each of his eight hands.'

Jamsgar Havvarson said, 'If I had my way, I would wipe this island clear of men and of cattle. Then I would take a spade and dig out the foundations and let it all sink into the sea; for it is a breeding-ground of wickedness.'

Thorfinn Thorfinnson said, 'That comes well from you, who have never dug your own garden in twenty years, but always make your wife do it.'

Jamsgar Havvarson said, 'I do not dig because I have a weak heart and bending down does not suit me. If you had a weak heart, you would understand better. Then you would see what injustice you do me.'

Gudbrod Gudbrodsson said, 'How can a man with a weak heart wield an axe as you do?'

Jamsgar Havvarson said, 'That is a secret told to me in a dream by a witch. I am under oath not to tell anyone else, especially you.'

Thorfinn Thorfinnson said, 'It is as good a way to avoid digging that I have heard of. When I get back home, I shall have such a dream and then I need dig no more. I am no lover of gardening, either!'

Jamsgar Havvarson said, 'You make light of a serious matter. When I have a moment to spare, I shall challenge you to fight and shall cut off your head for those words.'

Harald Sigurdson said, 'If you fools don't stop arguing, I shall fling you all overboard now, and let you swim home to Norway. Then you will see what a weak heart is like.'

Gudbrod Gudbrodsson said, 'It is all one to me. I can walk on the water, didn't you hear? And so can Thorfinn Thorfinnson. We both learned to do it at the same time. We went to a school run by a Russian witch in a cave near the mouth of the Dnieper. We paid good money to learn the trick. I have often wondered when the chance to practise on real water would occur, for up to the present we have only been able to do it on dry land, though we know exactly what to do on water.'

Harald went away then, for he knew that Norsemen would keep up this silly sort of talk for hours at a stretch, until they became so drunk with words that they would draw swords and hit each other, just to prove a point, or leap into the sea for a wager.

Chapter 5 *Haakon Redeye*

That night they slept again upon the ship, watching the fires burning high on the hilltops, afraid to go ashore lest such lawless men as they had already met surrounded them and killed them as they slept.

They woke at early dawn-time to find *Long Snake* half full of brackish water, from a hole in her side which needed caulking.

And as they lay, half-settled on a sandbank, filling that hole with rope strands and tarring it over, a longship swept out from behind them, down the inlet, and set course to the west.

Seeing their plight, the ship came close to them, within an arrow-flight, and then Harald saw that Haakon Redeye was in the prow, smiling at them in mockery.

'If I had more time,' he said, 'I would stay and help you, Sigurdson. But as it is I am behind time and must go on to visit my old grandmother who lives among the trolls. It is her birthday soon, and I have promised to take her a present. So you will forgive me, I am sure, if I do not stay to help!'

His men lined the side of the longship, grinning above the shields, and waving in derision.

Harald called out, 'Stay and fight like a man. I will meet you on board your own ship, bringing only two men with me. But at least give me the chance of my revenge.'

Haakon Redeye said, 'No thank you, Sigurdson. I have no wish to be struck by such as you. I have just eaten my breakfast, and it would be a waste of good food to go and get killed now. Goodbye !'

So Haakon's longship passed away out of sight, while Harald and his men swore furiously, baling out the water and caulking the hole in *Long Snake*'s side.

And when this was finished two hours later, a party went ashore and filled the empty beer barrels with fresh spring water, while others found a herd of sheep and took eight of them, having frightened away the shepherd boy by waving axes at him.

So they struggled back to their ship with the casks and the carcasses, into which they rubbed salt immediately, so that the meat would stay reasonably fresh for the voyage they had to make now to the west.

At last, when the sun was sinking and the tarred side

seemed to keep out the water, *Long Snake* set forth again in the track of Haakon Redeye.

And Harald said at sunset, 'I don't know where we are going, my comrades, but it would ill become such men as us to turn back now and become the laughing-stock of our women, when we are so close on the heels of the man who has done us such harm.'

They all agreed, cold as they were; and so the chase went on.

Chapter 6 Westering

Ever afterwards, until it came for them to go through the oaken doorway into Valhalla, where the old warriors sat at the long table smiling and waiting for them, the men of *Long Snake* remembered their journey to the west like a bad black dream.

Sometimes the deep green sea rose above them higher than a tall cliff face, then seemed to hang over them like a dark cloud before it thundered down onto them, smashing them to the boards, smiting the longship like a stick of wood in a waterfall, swirling it round and round again, until the creatures on board lost all sense of direction, all sense of the world, all sense of themselves.

Then they might be in the clear again, rolling and bucking on the great tides, as though they ran some mad sledge race down dreamlike slopes of green death, baling half-dazed with the sea-water in their rusty helmets, fighting a losing battle always against a sea that washed as it willed over their sides.

In ten leagues they had lost their mast and sail. In twenty leagues they had lost all knowledge of their names. Speech would not come to their frozen lips. They moved like men in a deep trance that could only end in death.

But by some miracle death did not come, yet.

Again and again he threatened, opening his wide foamy jaws as though to munch up *Long Snake*. And then he withdrew. . . .

And once Harald saw Haakon Redeye's longship, rolling far before them on a tide like the side of a green mountain, stumbling like a stallion with an arrow in its heart.

But he told no one. Indeed, for a while he could not recall the name of the man who sailed in her, the man he had set forth to destroy. It was like that, in those days of the journey; men forgot what their task was, the object of their journey, the name of their blood-enemy. . . .

And then, when it seemed that even death would be better than such voyaging, the sky cleared and the white birds came down again over the rocking boat, and the tall seas grew smooth as glass for a time – a sheet of glass as broad as the world, as muscular as a giant's flank.

And one evening, towards dusk, Long Snake grated beside a skerry, a low heap of rocks set lonely in the vastness of the seas. Then every man who had the power of speech leapt ashore shouting, dragging at the ropes with feeble hands to bring the longship to anchor.

And there, on that lonely skerry, with the darkness coming down over them like a grey cloak, the vikings broke up a barrel and struck flint to iron and somehow made themselves a fire to sit about.

In the depths of the oceans the men of the Long Snake sat on that tiny isle and tried to remember the names of the ten men they had lost in the days of storm-wrack. But before they could bring their brine-sodden brains to bear upon this business, the white birds came down upon them out of the darkness, sweeping them with their wings; and then a man screamed out, 'To the ship! To the ship! This island is sinking!'

Then they knew that the water was up to their knees,

and then to their waists. They saw their fire swamped and the little skerry fall into blackness.

And those who still had strength of arm and speed of mind struck out in the wild waves to where the longship wrestled with its ropes.

That night five more men were lost, and over the creaking, leaking, battered longship the sea birds whirled and cried like mocking furies.

Harald said, as he lay by the shield-wall, 'It ill becomes any man to lead his fellows so far out into the hidden seas on so bootless a quest. Once again, Grummoch, I have done wrong.'

Giant Grummoch sprawled, groaning in the scuppers, but turned his great matted head to say, 'Harald Sigurdson, no man may see into the future. No man may choose his fate. His life egg is held in ghostly hands and is outside his reach.'

But others, such as Gudbrod Gudbrodsson, muttered that in the old days it was the duty of a chieftain to let himself be sacrificed when his people fell on evil days. Another man, who lay beside him, said that Harald owed this to his henchmen, who had left their homes to sail with him on his voyage of revenge.

Grummoch shouted above the rising wind to them, telling them that they had left no homes, since there were no homes to leave after Haakon's visitation with fire; and that the revenge they sought was not Harald's alone, but equally their own.

The grumbling stopped then, and Grummoch crawled to the axe-chest, where all the weapons were stowed away from the salt-water, greased with mutton-fat and wrapped about with cloths. He took from this chest his

own axe, *Death Kiss*, which he held before him now and said, 'I am oath-brother to Harald Sigurdson and it is both my duty and my right to stay by his side. Let any three of you come forward now and hold an axe conference with me to settle this argument.'

But no one stirred, then or the next day. And the day after that, as *Long Snake* ran in among a shoal of rocky outcrops, they saw such a thing as took all thought of mutiny from their minds.

Lolling lazily between two pointed rocks, the dark green weed already dragging about it, was the prow of a longship, its bow-post carved in the shape of a dragon's head with teeth of walrus bone.

Beside it on a rock lay an axe, already brown with salt-rust.

Harald gazed over the side and said, 'The man who burned my village has time a-plenty to consider his wickedness now.'

As they ran past Haakon's longship, Gudbrod Gudbrodsson said, 'Mother Sea punished him, Harald; what more is left for us to do?'

Harald said, 'What can we do, but sit here in this ship, our helmets in our hands, to bale out water? Both sail and oars have gone now. Do you expect me to turn *Long Snake* about by magic and guide her back to our fjord?'

As he spoke, a long low coastline jutted jagged over the green horizon, and a wind freshened and drove *Long Snake* onwards towards it.

Harald said, 'That is your answer, Gudbrod Gudbrodsson. We go where the Fates send us; and the Fates send us to a land no man has ever spoken of before.'

And it was in this manner that *Long Snake* at last came to the land which men called Greenland in after years.

Chapter 7 *Innuit*

Long Snake landed under the beetling crags in late Spring. By late summer the men who were left, thirty of them, had gathered driftwood from the swirling fjords and had made a new mast and new oars, clumsy but fit for use on the high seas by men whose hands were stronger than most.

Out of stones and driftwood, turfs and the skins of whale, walrus and bear, they made their sleeping-bags and hangings, for they were able men with the needle, and each man carried his own sewing-case of deerhide filled with needles – of hard-wood, hare's tooth, fishbone. It would ill become a viking, they said, to have to go home to his wife every time his breeches needed patching !

For food they ate what meat they could come by, even fox, though this did not please some of the younger warriors who had been brought up delicately on a diet of pig and sheep.

Yet one day, in private council, Harald said to Grummoch, 'This goes well enough for men who are born at the outer edge of the world; but I have noticed that a chill wind blows down from the north these last two mornings, and with it comes the smell of snow. Stay we here a month longer and I give it as my opinion that this fjord will become icebound, and what few roots and berries we can find will be hidden with a thick blanket of snow from our eyes and hands.'

Grummoch said, 'Last night I heard the howling of dogs, which I did not like. I went to the brow of the little hill, above the strange humped mounds, and saw a long line of dogs racing away to the west. Not the dogs of our country, but big round-bodied dogs, carrying much fur and running with their tails curled up, in a most undog-like manner.'

'Running in lines?' asked Harald Sigurdson, amazed.

Grummoch nodded his great shaggy head. 'In lines,' he repeated. 'As though they followed a leader. And I will tell you more, Harald oath-brother, though I beg you not to tell the others, lest they call me a madman and pelt me with bones; it seemed to me, in the moonlight, that these dogs ran with two-footed creatures, hardly men, but more like trolls.'

Harald said, 'Describe them, friend, for this is most interesting – more interesting than the lays which Thorfinn skald makes up about the fire at night :

> The brown snake glides the green hillocks,
> Seeking the red-eyed wolf;
> But, finding wolf rock-battered, makes
> Its resting-place above the weed-clogged fjord.

That was his last one, meant to tell our story.'

Grummoch snorted. 'It is rubbish,' he said. 'I have known byre-boys to make better songs about the names of their cattle. In Orkney once, I heard a man sing this . . .'

But Harald stopped him and said, 'Another time, oath-brother. That song will wait, but your news must not grow cold. Tell me about the trolls who ran with the dogs last night.'

Grummoch snorted a little, but put on a good face as a

viking should, though angry, and said, 'You will not believe me when I tell you that these trolls seemed hardly
taller than my waist, but as thick round as my own body.
Their heads were great and round and covered with fur.
They made no sound as they ran with the dogs. I think
they carried spears, but I am not sure now.'

Harald answered, 'We have fought the men of Frankland and Spain, and also the men of Miklagard. We have
outwitted the wild horsemen who ride along the Dnieper.
It would ill become us to grow fearful of small trolls with
furry heads who run with curly-tailed dogs in the moonlight, think you?'

Grummoch said, 'It depends on their numbers, and on
the strength of their magic. However strong a viking, he
must not hope to struggle on if fifty trolls smother him.
Nor can any man, viking or not, as is shown in the saga
of Olaf Skragge, lift axe against magic, if it is brewed and
cast the right way. It is my counsel that we should lie
with our swords at our sides by night, and that we should
sleep with one ear open.'

Harald laughed and said, 'Man who sleeps not, fights
not. If the trolls come, then we must take our chance; but
we must not frighten ourselves to death, lying in wait for
them. Look, friend, I counsel that tomorrow we begin to
caulk *Long Snake* in readiness for a voyage back home,
while the seas are still free of ice. Others can go hunting
for meat so that we may feed well on the journey. Then,
if we are lucky, we might sail before the wind changes
and before the week is out. What say you?'

Grummoch nodded. 'We cannot sail too soon for some
of the men. This daily diet of fish and snow-bear meat is
making them unwell. Their skin is dry and flaking with

the salt, and many of them have such boils on back and
buttocks that they will not find the task of rowing a joy-
ful one. Yes, let us go at the first chance.'

When they went back to the men, they found them sitting about the fires, grumbling and wishing they could
see their wives and children again.

Thorfinn skald was standing in the firelight, chanting
the latest song he had made, to amuse them:

> 'Danish men have great big feet;
> Reindeer meat is good to eat;
> Irishmen have long red noses;
> What can equal the smell of roses?
>
> I have met a man who can
> Swallow the biggest cooking-pan;
> I have met a man who knows
> A man who knows
> A man who knows
> A white-eyed king with twenty toes,
> And on each toe a white-eyed cat –
> And what do you think of that?'

Grummoch said, 'I think very little, friend! Now listen
to sense, my fellows. Our leader, Harald Sigurdson, has
news that will interest you more than this stuff of Thorfinn's cat!'

So Harald sat by the fire and explained to the vikings
what his plan was, and they all agreed, though some who
still bore the scars of their last voyage expressed the hope
that this time things would go better.

Thorfinn sulked in a corner, and the young ones called
out, 'Pussy! Pussy!' to him, while others mewed like
cats.

It was while they all sat listening to Harald, and arguing among themselves, as shipmen always do before a voyage, that Grummoch suddenly looked up and gave a cry of surprise, pointing into the dusk.

All men followed his finger and then they, too, gave cries of surprise, and their thoughts of voyaging faded to the backs of their minds as snow fades when the first sun of Spring breathes down upon the northern hills.

Round them, just beyond the firelight, stood men – but such strange men that none of the vikings had seen their like.

They were as short as dwarfs and their faces, ringed round with fur, were broad and flat and yellow. The eyes that they looked from were little more than slits in the skin of their faces, and their mouths were broad.

Each one was round in the body and wore the skin of the white snow-bear. Each one carried a short lance tipped with narwhal bone, cruelly barbed.

There were many of these men, perhaps a hundred, and behind them stood dogs, hundreds of dogs, all staring silent and green-eyed at the vikings round the fire.

Harald said, 'Here are your trolls, Grummoch. I would like to see the hero who could take on this lot, even with his axe – and our weapons are all in the hut, where we cannot reach them easily.'

Grummoch began to rise, lazily, saying, 'I will go amongst them and kill a few dozen of them with my bare hands. Then perhaps they will go away.'

But even as the giant got to his knees, six of the trolls stepped forward noiselessly, and levelled their harpoons at his breast, without speaking, without a change of expression on their flat, slit-eyed faces.

Grummoch sat down again, thinking twice of his pre-
vious offer now.

Then, at last, a wizened troll shuffled forward, his
thick legs ragged with hare-skins and deerhide. He carried
in his hand a club made of the jawbone of a narwhal, set
with the tusk of a walrus so that the weapon looked most
formidable.

He went from viking to viking, gazing at each one
carefully, as though he had not seen their like before.

Close behind him walked four great dogs, with curly
tails, and these creatures sniffed at every man the troll
halted by.

The vikings did not move, but sat as still as stones. No
one liked that war-club, or those sniffing dogs with fierce

eyes and curly tails. But Harald signalled to them with
his eyes to remain seated and not to offend the troll or his
dogs.

Then, at last, the old troll went back to his many followers and began to talk to them in a strange harsh voice,
using many small words and waving his club at each
pause.

Someone in the crowd of trolls started to beat on a
small drum, and then the trolls began to prance round
the fire, slowly, like creatures in a bad dream, waving
their harpoons as they went.

At last, when the sweat was standing out on the brow
of every viking, the strange dance stopped, and the old
troll came forward once again.

He stood in the firelight and tapped his broad chest
with the flat of his hand, saying, 'Jaga! Kaga! Jaga!
Kaga!'

Grummoch said, 'I think he is telling us his name. Tell
him yours, oath-brother.'

So Harald stood up, slowly and gently, so as not to
draw the harpoons upon himself. Then he too patted his
chest and said, 'Harald Sigurdson! Harald Sigurdson!'

The troll listened, but did not seem to understand. So
Harald spoke his name again and again, until it began
to sound most foolish and he wondered why the Gods
had given it to him.

But at last the old troll seemed to understand, and said,
pointing at Harald, 'Rold Sgun! Rold Sgun! Rold Sgun!'

Harald nodded, smiling, making the best of a bad job.

Then the old troll swept his furry hand round to indi-
cate his followers.

'Innuit,' he said. 'Innuit.'

Grummoch whispered, 'He is telling us that the trolls call themselves Innuit, Harald.'

Harald said, 'Aye, that much had occurred even to me, friend. But who makes the next move?'

There was little need to ask, for the question was soon answered. The old troll began to bark like a seal out on a Spring fjord, and immediately the Innuit rushed forward and took the vikings, binding their arms with thongs of deerhide so swiftly that no man had the chance of defending himself.

Harald said, 'These men, if men they be, move faster then any I have known, even the men of Miklagard – and they are brisk little devils!'

So it was that Harald Sigurdson and the vikings with him were captured by the Innuit, just when they planned to sail away from Greenland in *Long Snake*.

Chapter 8 *The Cooking-Place*

Never did the vikings forget their long journey to the north, bound down upon sledges and dragged by dogs; or sitting bundled up in long skin-boats, always nosing northwards round the nesses and along the black fjords.

The Innuit treated them well, pushing blubber into their mouths, whether they wanted it or not; and wrapping them in bear-pelts when the early darkness fell.

The old troll, Jaga-Kaga, often came and looked down at them and touched their long hair, comparing it with his own thick grey locks, or the coarse black hair of his younger followers. Then he would nod and go away, shaking his head, puzzled. Once he went round lifting the vikings' eyelids, and staring into their pale eyes at a close distance, as though he thought they were sightless.

Gudbrod Gudbrodsson said, 'Never did I meet a man who smelt so like a bear before.'

Thorfinn Thorfinnson said, 'Never did I travel so slowly. These trolls take a week to go the distance we can go in one day, in and out the fjords with their strange boats.'

Always where the Innuit rested for the night, they built little cairns of stones, under which they laid blubber and fish, so that their hunting-fellowship would have something to eat should they need to make the return journey southwards again.

The vikings, used to salt fish and fire-dried meat, could

not stomach so much blubber at first, and many of them were sick when made to eat half-rotten grouse, with the skin still on it, and uncooked.

But being sick did not save them, for immediately the old troll barked like a seal at his followers and they ran forward with more half-rotten grouse, so that their prisoners should not go hungry.

Grummoch said, 'When I get back to Norway, I shall eat no more meat, cooked or uncooked. Nor shall I look a fish in the eye again. But I shall eat only barley bread and drink only fresh milk, straight from the cow's udder.'

Harald said, 'At the edge of the world, it ill becomes a man to speak of what he will do in the future. Mayhap there will be no future but this, for evermore. Only blubber and rotten grouse and skin-boats and stone hovels. Only that!'

'Then,' said Grummoch, 'I hope that these trolls will stick their harpoons in me soon, for I am not the sort of man who likes living with dogs and eating birds with their feathers on.'

Grummoch said this because when they came at last to the great cooking-place of the Innuit, all the vikings were pushed into a long low hut of stone, together with the dogs, who snapped and snarled almost unceasingly.

The ground was as hard as iron, and now each night there came such a bitter frost that the men were glad of the dogs, who slept on them and kept the cold from them, to some degree.

Then the snow began to fall. The vikings watched it through the little window-holes. It fell like an immense shower of feathers from the white breast of the swan, until it lay taller than a man, and then the long hut was buried deep.

But the Innuit did not seem to notice this, and carried on hunting and dancing and drum-playing as though it were summer and not the start of a hard winter.

They dug a tunnel to the long hut and passed back and forth, bringing blubber and lamp-oil to fill the little soapstone lamps, which gave a dim and smoky light and made the vikings cough.

The women of the Innuit came too, to gaze at the white-faced strangers with blue crystal eyes. These women were dressed exactly like the men, in skins, with a fur hood about their heads. But they were quiet-voiced gentle creatures, who simply squatted down among the dogs and smiled at the Northmen, without speaking to them.

One day, as a great delicacy, a party of these Innuit women brought in a stone dish of hot seals' liver and sat down while the vikings ate it.

This made some of them feel sick, but they did not show their queasiness in case it offended the Innuit women, who went to great pains to see that each viking had the same amount of food as his fellow.

Grummoch said, 'They think we are dogs. Harald. You notice, they see that each dog gets his fair share, and so they do with us.'

Harald said, 'I do not care what they think we are, if only they would let us move about, outside this hut. I have begun to dream of huts and dogs, every night now. It is becoming unbearable. If they do not do something, I

can feel that I shall run berserk, and that would be un-
lucky for them.'

Grummoch said, 'Yesterday when I was watching
through the little window-hole on the side where the
snow is thinnest, I saw a young troll strike an older one.
They were arguing about hot seals' liver. It was only
the lightest blow, but it was a blow, nevertheless.'

Harald said, 'What happened then, oath-brother?'

Grummoch said, 'Ten of the others ran up and stripped off the young one's fur clothes. Then they bound him
hand and foot with reindeer thongs and merely laid him
out in the snow. He did not cry out, but just lay, smiling.
This morning the snow had covered him deeply. He will
be seen no more until the Spring thaw, I would say.
And this is what would happen if you ran berserk, my
friend.'

Harald said, 'If only I had my sword, *Peace-giver*, I
would risk what they did with me after I had struck the
first blow. But our swords and axes lie in the weapon-hut
near *Long Snake* still. These trolls did not seem inter-
ested in them, or in the longship. It is strange.'

Grummoch answered, 'They are a strange little folk.
Almost like men, yet not quite men.'

Harald said, 'What did the young one look like, the
one they laid in the snow, when they had stripped all the
fur covering from him?'

And Grummoch said, 'Just like any other man, save
that his skin was yellowish in colour. It seems to me that
only their faces are different from those of proper men.
It is their thick bundles of clothes that make them look
like trolls. Their arms and legs are as well-formed as our
own, and their bodies are much sleeker and plumper,

since they feed so well, in a desert land that would not seem to provide food for a moderately-sized mouse!'

That night the big dog who was the leader of all the others leapt at Grummoch's throat as he squatted over the fire, for no reason at all. Grummoch was compelled to deal with this dog in a final manner, lest the other dogs followed their leader and killed all the vikings.

It was not the sort of work which the giant enjoyed. Nor did he like to see the other dogs tearing at the body of their dead leader.

But when it was all over, Harald said to him, 'Now the dogs have elected you as their king, Grummoch. Look how they sit about you with their lolling tongues and bright eyes, as though they are asking you to tell them what they must do next.'

Grummoch said, 'I never hoped to become the king of the dogs. It ill becomes a viking to talk bark-language, yet who can hold off his fate? And in any case, these dogs might be useful to us, in such a case as we are at present.'

Grummoch got up then and went to the thick wooden door and began to scratch at it, pretending to bite at its edges.

Immediately the pack of dogs jostled each other to do the same, pushing Grummoch aside as though they considered it beneath the dignity of their new king to perform so menial a task.

Claw and tooth worked without ceasing, until at last the fierce dogs had broken through the hide strapping which held the planks together and then the door fell to pieces.

The dogs stood back so that their king could pass down the long snow tunnel that led to the outside world.

Grummoch bent low and crawled through the tunnel. The other vikings made to follow him, but the dogs turned on them with a snarl, bidding them hold back, for they considered themselves the king's bodyguard and must follow after him.

Thorfinn Thorfinnson said wryly, 'It ill becomes a viking to stick his nose into business which does not concern him. I am content to wait until my dog-brothers give me leave to pass through.'

Gudbrod Gudbrodsson said, 'If I had my spear, *Tickler*, I would show these dogs what a viking can do when he gives his mind to it – but, alas, my own teeth and nails would match but poorly with those of my new furry comrades!'

Jamsgar Havvarson said, 'I do not care now what happens, as long as these dogs do not expect me to run on all fours with them and grow a curly tail.'

Thorfinn Thorfinnson said, 'A curly tail is all you need to complete your equipment, for I have always thought you to resemble a dog rather than anything else.'

Gudbrod Gudbrodsson said, 'The sooner the Innuit lay you two out in the snow, the better; for there are two sorts of men I cannot abide – fools and bad poets.'

Harald Sigurdson said, 'If you three do not hold your peace, I will be compelled to act towards you as Svend Tryvlye acted towards the Lappland giant, and put my toe under your seats with a vengeance.'

Then they were quiet, because Harald Sigurdson was said to have the best kicking-toe in Norway, as he had shown once when attacked without his sword by a bull. That bull had not dared to sit down for a week afterwards, and had attacked no one since. Some men said that this showed how wise a bull he was; others had said that it bore testimony to Harald's kicking-toe.

So the vikings stopped arguing and followed the last of the dogs down the dark snow tunnel, into the space before the long ice-house of the Innuit.

And there the Innuit were ranged behind their old troll leader, their bone arrows drawn to the head and pointing at the Northmen. The faces of the Innuit were fierce and stiff like stone, so that the Northmen began to think twice about rushing forward any further.

But when Grummoch and the dogs stood in the open, with their breath rising like ghosts out of their mouths because of the cold, the old troll leader held up his hand to his followers and they lowered their vicious little bows. But their faces were still fierce and stiff like stone.

Then the troll leader shuffled forward and patted Grummoch on the chest, as though he were a good dog – to do which he had to stretch up on tiptoe for there was a great difference in the height of the two men.

Then all the Innuit shuffled forward and did the same, and bent and did the same to the dogs, who now sat with dangling tongues in the snow about Grummoch.

'Odin be praised!' said Gudbrod Gudbrodsson. 'For at last we are accepted as being trustworthy dogs!'

Thorfinn said, 'That is well, unless they expect us to eat bones and pull sledges!'

Harald said, 'Remember the bull I once met on the fells above Jagesgard!'

So they did not start another discussion.

Now the vikings were invited into the long ice-house of the trolls, among the men and the dogs, and the many women.

This ice-house was buried deep under the snow and all its window-holes were stopped up with rolls of walrus hides. Twenty soapstone lamps burned there, and the place was extremely hot. Nor was the air made sweeter by the stack of seal carcasses and dried fish which stood in one corner. Harald blew down his nostrils for a while, then said to Grummoch, 'Friend, this reminds me of the sweat-baths in Finnmark, but there they do not store fish and blubber as well.'

Grummoch said, 'I care not how this place smells. At least it is better than being in prison in the dog-house. Freedom is a lovely state, Harald. At least a viking can die with a quiet mind when he knows that he is free.'

Harald said, 'I wish all you fellows would stop talking of dying, as though it is the prize most sought after in life. I want to live, and to see my two sons and my dear wife, Asa, again.'

Grummoch said, 'When I lived in Caledonia on my mother's steading, and before I took service with King MacMiorog of Dun-an-oir, I was a pleasant enough fellow, and thought only of playing upon the flute and kissing the girls at the Wednesday barn-feasts. In those days I never spoke of death, for my mind was set upon making my fortune, and having great adventures. But now that I have had adventures a-plenty, and now that I know that few men make fortunes and keep them, I do not mind contemplating the possibility of death, which under certain circumstances, could become a restful state of being.'

Harald said, 'I shall not argue with you any longer, for this is a fool's topic. I shall only correct you by saying that a state of being belongs to live men, and that dead men are in a state of no-being.'

Never were there such argumentative men as were in the Northlands at that time. They would sit on a rock with the sea rising about them and argue about life and death until they were drowned. Indeed, in the village of Wadnesdon, just south of Kellsfjord, eight vikings had been burnt to death only that year as they sat about the feast-board arguing about which leg of the table would be burned off first when the fire spread.

Now in the ice-house all was bustle and blubber-eating. The women ran here and there and pushed gobbets of the shiny fat into the mouths of their guests.

And after a while the Innuit men began to take off their heavy fur clothes, because of the great heat, until they wore only a little strip of seal-hide about them. Soon the vikings did likewise, for this was the hottest place they had ever known.

Then the Innuit men and women admired the wolves and bears and dragons which many of the Northmen had tattooed upon their chests or backs, tracing them with their little yellow fingers in wonder.

Grummoch, who had the great snake of Midgard etched on his broad chest, was an object of especial wonder. He was also very ticklish. So it was that before long most of the young Innuit folk swarmed about him to hear him laughing as he rolled on the floor among the fish bladders and seal-skins, trying to escape the roguish fingers.

The dogs became so worried at seeing their new leader treated in such a manner that they began to snarl, and had to be driven back to their dog-house with walrus-hide whips, lest they attacked the Innuit on Grummoch's behalf.

And that evening was a very merry one for all, especially when the vikings discovered that the Innuit had a store of stone jars full of red berry-juice, which had much the same flavour as their own bramble wine back at home above the fjord.

The next day, since Grummoch had seemed to desert them by sleeping in the ice-house, the dogs disowned him as their king and fought among each other to elect another king.

Grummoch was not sorry about this, for he little looked forward to learning bark-language, which seemed to him a mighty difficult form of speech, especially since it often must be accompanied with waggings of the tail, or suchlike antics, of which he felt himself largely incapable.

Learning the Innuit language was bad enough, in that long winter about the fire with the blubber-lamps smoking and the fish-stack getting riper and riper.

Yet there was this consolation, that the Innuit had very few words, and by and by the vikings made a fair show at saying what they wished in the Innuit tongue; though they made many errors in pronunciation, of course. Yet the Innuit women were always most patient and repeated words again and again, until even Jamsgar Havvarson, who was slow-witted, had picked up the main words.

Not only did the vikings learn the Innuit language; they also learned to run with the hunting-fellowship and spear seals and walruses on the frozen sea. Often they would run for mile after mile in the moonlight, for there was no day now at all, to where they had heard there was a family of seals. And then they would help carry back the load to the cooking-place, and be rewarded by the Innuit women with hot seals' liver.

Grummoch said once, 'My next task will be to learn the seal language, which should not be difficult since I have eaten so much seal-meat that I am more than half a seal myself.'

But he did not do that. Instead, he killed a white bear.

This happened quite by accident, since, if Grummoch had known it was going to happen, it wouldn't have happened at all. He was not so great a fool as that.

One day, Grummoch was down in a bear-pit, setting the sharp stakes of whalebone so that when the Innuit had covered the hole with seal-skin and snow, a white bear might fall down there and be spiked, since this hole was dug on the white bear tracks.

Suddenly Grummoch was aware that there were no Innuit up above to hand down the whalebone stakes. Then he saw that a great white bear, as tall as himself, was looking down at him, waving its head about on a neck as lithe as a snake.

Grummoch was never a man to refuse battle to anyone, bear or not, but this time he felt at a loss since he had nothing but a whalebone stake to defend himself with. Nevertheless, he told the bear to come on down and to see who was the better man, or the better bear, whichever way the bear chose to regard this challenge. And when the bear did not answer in good Norse, Grummoch tried him with Celtic; and still the bear only stood there and waved his head and showed his curved white teeth as though asking Grummoch to praise their sharpness and whiteness.

'Nay,' said Grummoch, 'you'll get no such praise from me, my lad. If you are such a fool as to stand up there, then I'll come up to you.'

This time Grummoch spoke in the Innuit tongue, for by now most of the vikings had become so used to hearing this language spoken that they used it constantly, even among themselves, since it would have been impolite to talk in Norse among their hosts, the Innuit trolls.

Well, it seemed that the white bear knew Innuit tongue, however lacking his learning in Norse and Celtic, because as soon as Grummoch made to get out of the hole, the bear began to climb into it, so that the two warriors met halfway and tumbled back into the hole, the bear being rather the heavier of them.

But though Grummoch was underneath, he realized that the narrowness of that hole worked to his advantage, and though he hated to take an unfair part in such a fight, he wasted little time in using his whalebone stake, which served as well as any other sort of sword, at close quarters.

There was much roaring on both sides for a while, during which the Innuit folk came back and stood over the hole to see what was happening down there, and perhaps to shoot a few arrows at the bear if the chance arose.

But Grummoch called on them not to loose forth their arrows in case one of them should go astray and pin him, too, to the ground.

In any case, the outfly of arrows was not needed, for within three minutes Grummoch eased himself from under the slumped bear and climbed up out of the hole.

'I have done my work for the day,' he said to Jaga-Kaga, the troll chieftain. 'Now send your young men down to bring up the bear.'

It took twelve Innuit to raise the great white carcass.

As for Grummoch, his arm and chest were deeply scored by the bear's claws, but otherwise he went scatheless. He laughed about these small scratches as he called them, but fell in a faint on the way back to the cooking-place. It took twelve Innuit to carry him, too; so Grummoch and the bear arrived on sledges at the same time, but it was Grummoch over whom the Innuit women made the greater moan, since they feared the bear's claws might have spoiled the beautiful tattooing on his chest.

After that, Grummoch was given the title of 'Bear Man'. He was also given the choice of any of the young Innuit women as his wife. But he declined this honour, saying that it would ill become a dainty little troll woman to wed such a hulking savage as himself, for he was a man of very bad habits and always went to bed with his boots on.

At this, there was much wailing among the Innuit girls, who now regarded him as something of a hero, but in the end they accepted his decision and instead gave him a necklace of fox's teeth, a sleeping-bag of seal-skin decorated with little blue beads made of soapstone, and a hatchet of walrus tooth, set in a haft of narwhal bone.

There is no knowing what adventures Grummoch might have had among the Innuit that winter, for the old witch-woman who flung the seal-bones to forecast the future had told them all that Grummoch was born to become a chieftain.

'Aye,' whispered Thorfinn Thorfinnson, who hadn't killed a bear, or anything bigger than a small seal, 'a chieftain of dogs, no doubt!'

This was meant to be a joke, but Thorfinn forgot himself and said the words in Innuit tongue, and the dogs heard him. When they had finished chasing him, he had no trousers left, and so the Northmen called him Thorfinn Breechless from that day on.

But Grummoch did not become a chieftain there, for one day, when the snow melted and the ice softened under the warm breath of the new Spring, a great kayak came into the fjord where the cooking-place was. And in it were two Innuit, but of another tribe. They were so thin that it seemed one could see through their skin down to their bones. And they were so weak that they sat in their kayak like dead men until they were lifted out and warmed by the fire in the ice-house.

And after a few hours, when they had gained strength through whale blubber and hot seals' liver, they told how they had been caught by the ice when the winter came on, and could not get back to their own cooking-places, and so had turned about and paddled to the south.

And there, after many many days of paddling, they said, was a great land of rivers and hills and much grass, and such creatures as they had never seen in the North-land, creatures with horns outside their heads and not in their mouths like the walrus.

And besides, there were men, but different Innuit from themselves, although some of their words were the same. They were red men, who grew feathers out of the tops of their heads, and had long noses and wore few clothes.

The two brothers from the kayak said that these red men were very big, almost as big as Grummoch, and most redoubtable fighters with their hatchets.

Gudbrod Gudbrodsson, always looking out to catch someone, said, 'The best hatchets are those made in Norway, for there we have the true iron which will hold an edge. The things you speak of must be toys, fit only for women to chop the kindling or for small boys to tease each other with.'

The man from the kayak said, 'In my boat you will find such axes as the red men use. See for yourselves.'

The vikings went out to the kayak, which lay in the fjord, and there, in a deerhide wrapping, they found the hatchets, which were of red metal and very sharp. They were set on painted staves and garnished with many-coloured feathers.

Grummoch said, 'These are wonderfully pretty things,

but too light for my taste. Yet, if I had a big one like these, there is no knowing what deeds I might perform.'

Harald said, 'You do well enough with a stake of whalebone, oath-brother!'

But Grummoch still said, 'I would like to meet these red men and bargain with them for an axe or two like these.'

Thorfinn Thorfinnson said, 'They might prove to be better bargainers than you, Grummoch Giant, and then where would you be?'

Grummoch said, 'Dead and happy, friend!'

And they could get no more sense out of him. But that night, while the others were admiring the bead necklaces and the copper bracelets that the two brothers had brought back, Grummoch spoke long with Jaga-Kaga, the chieftain of the trolls, urging him to let the vikings go south and sail *Long Snake* again, towards this land which the brothers had visited.

At first the old man shook his head and wept, saying that he loved the vikings like his own family now that he had got to know them. But in the end, Grummoch prevailed upon him, and he consented to let them go, provided they would come back and stay with him again.

So the Innuit carried the vikings southwards on their sledges and there they found *Long Snake*, just as they had left her, and all their weapons in the little hut they had built.

And so they set off in the Spring once more, with a wind behind them to fill out their seal-skin sail.

Thorfinn Thorfinnson said, 'If I go back to the Innuit, may Odin claim my head!'

Gudbrod Gudbrodsson said, 'Odin would get small

profit out of your head, for it is full of blubber, like your fat stomach !'

Harald Sigurdson said, 'Remember the bull I met on the fells above Jagesgard. Remember my famous kicking-toe !'

Then they were all silent, and did nothing but wave to the weeping Innuit, who stood along the shore nodding their furry heads. Even the dogs seemed sad to see Grummoch and his pack go from the Northland, for they sat in the slushy grass with their noses between their paws, and whined in a way they had never done before.

Chapter **10** *Landfall*

Spring was at its full when *Long Snake* first turned her nose towards new land.

The vikings had spoken of hardly anything except axes, bead-work, and helmets of feathers since they had set forth from Greenland. Sometimes, it is true, they had remembered Norway; but most often that memory had been pushed from their minds by some other thought, to do with the land they were to find.

Harald said to Grummoch, 'If there is gold in this land, we stand fair chance of making that fortune which you say few men make.'

And Grummoch had answered, 'Gold was buried in the earth and in the streams to tempt mankind; that is my thought. Whoso takes gold must often take death with it. Consider the case of Thorwald Niklasson of Jomsby, who found a whole box of gold in Frankland and got it back to his own fjord, only to have his throat cut by a little man who hid in a tree, waiting for his longship to make landfall.'

Harald said, 'Nay, lad, I shall consider the case of Grummoch and of Harald Sigurdson, who are brisk enough fellows not to be caught napping by fellows in trees! Besides, Thorwald Niklasson of Jomsby was a beef-headed fool to take gold from a church of the Frankish Whitechrist, for that was holy gold. And the man who cut his throat was sent by the Frankish priests to impress that point upon him.'

Grummoch said, 'It was not the point they impressed upon him, but the edge! And the edge seems to have been very sharp, according to men I know, who saw the situation Thorwald Niklasson was in afterwards.'

Then they sighted land, great stretches of it, and all green.

Jamsgar Havvarson said, 'Hardly ever have my eyes so relished the sight of land, and I am nigh on thirty and have made the sea my trade. But after weeks of sailing – and I grant the winds have been good ones, right from the wide mouth of Freya, bless her! – I am less than anxious to eat another mouthful of raw fish or of blubber, or to drink another cupful of brackish Greenland water or berry beer.'

Gudbrod Gudbrodsson replied, 'A true viking is a beast without a belly. A true viking can live for weeks on one breath of salt air. A true viking thinks more of voyaging than of victuals.'

Then Thorfinn Thorfinnson said, 'Then a true viking must be a fool, for there is scarcely anything so desirable as good roast pork and barley bread spread thick with butter, and a flagon of well-fermented beer to wash it down with.'

Harald broke into this conversation to say, 'I am a little more than surprised to hear a skald praising so highly the pleasures of eating and drinking. It had been my notion that poets thought only of cloudy heavens where old warriors lay back upon their shields and listened to the Snow Maidens singing endless songs of adventures.'

Thorfinn said, 'A poet must live, Harald.'

Gudbrod said, 'Why?'

Then they drove in towards land.

'I name that long stretch Helleland, that other stretch Markland – and the piece that lies far behind it Vinland – for I am certain that grapes grow there, as they do at Miklagard, it looks so sunny and so rich,' said Harald Sigurdson, pointing.

'And what do you name the boat which is coming towards us over the billows?' asked Grummoch, taking the axe from his belt.

Harald gazed towards a long narrow boat, hardly more than a thin shell, with a high prow and high stern. In it five men paddled swiftly and in rhythm. They were bare to the waist and wore feathers in their black hair. They were now little more than two bowshots from *Long Snake*, for they had moved fast in the trough of the seas and had been hidden for so long.

Harald said, 'I name that the boat of welcome,' but loosened his sword in his belt, all the same.

Now the canoe came so close that any man on *Long Snake* could have thrown his helmet into it with little trouble. And the vikings saw that the men in it were reddish in the colour of their skin – or, perhaps, a little inclined to the hue of copper.

'These are Innuit of a different sort,' said Gudbrod. 'Try them in the Innuit tongue, Harald, for I doubt they understand good Norse.'

Slowly Harald called out, 'What men are you, friends?' cupping his hand about his mouth.

A red man stood up in the narrow boat. His chest was covered with yellow streaks and his arms were heavy with arm-bands. He carried a long spear in his right hand, at one end of which was a tuft of feathers, dyed red.

This man threw back his head and in a high nasal voice answered, 'Beothuk! Beothuk! Ha! Ha! Ha!'

Then he poised himself and flung the spear. It struck, quivering, in the dragon prow of *Long Snake*.

'That is a bad omen and a good throw,' said Grummoch. 'These Beothuk seem to be less than friendly, Harald.'

Harald answered, 'Perhaps they are simple folk, like Lapplanders and English. I will talk to them again.'

Once more he cupped his hands and said slowly, 'We are friends from the north.'

The next spear stuck in the mast of *Long Snake*, a hand's breadth from Harald's head.

Grummoch said, 'Aye, simple folk – but good warriors, also like the Lapplanders and the English!'

Now the canoe circled *Long Snake* and then set off again for the shore, the red men laughing as they paddled.

Gudbrod said, 'It seems to me that if all the men of Markland are of one mind, we shall meet with little to laugh about.'

But Jamsgar said, 'Pooh! Look at this spear-point. It is blunted by sticking into our prow. If a piece of oak can ruin a weapon, these cannot be such fearful warriors.'

Grummoch patted him on the shoulder gently so that Jamsgar almost fell to the deck.

'Your ribs are not of oak, my friend,' he said. 'And though this metal may be soft, yet it is hard enough to send you out on the long journey that ends in Valhalla. Bear that in mind.'

Jamsgar said ruefully, 'I shall bear in mind that when Grummoch praises a man with his hand, the man is never the same again. I can scarcely lift my arm now.'

Harald said, 'All the same, we are hungry and thirsty. We shall run ashore for a while at least, in what we call Markland. Mayhap all will be well, after all.'

Long Snake headed for a strip of sandy shore. As the vikings drew closer, they saw that the shore was thick with red men, and that each of them carried a weapon of some sort – hatchet, spear or club.

Grummoch said to his fellows, 'Have courage, friends, and put on your helmets with the bull's horns, for that may impress these folk.'

Gudbrod said, 'That is scarcely likely, giant. I can see three of the red men wearing bull's horns, too. And what's more, they have eagle's feathers to go with them! We have not eagle's feathers!'

Harald said grimly, sword in hand, 'I have yet to hear that a bunch of feathers can improve a man's swordplay or his strength, and these seem to be without swords, and to be smaller men than we are.'

'Hm!' thought Thorfinn to himself, 'but there are many more of them.'

Chapter II *First Meeting*

As *Long Snake* ran into the shallows, Harald called out to the vikings, 'Make no threatening gestures, fellows, but be ready. If they wish for peace, it would ill become such hungry wolves as ourselves to deny it to them. But if they wish for war, then see that each stroke finds its mark, and none of that silly flailing of the axe that Danish men are given to. There are more of them than of us, and every stroke must bite.'

As they leaped overboard, into the waist-high waters, the air was full of the whirring of arrows, and many of the vikings feared for their lives. But it was noticed that the feathered shafts stuck into the strakes of *Long Snake* and hit no one.

'They are simply testing us,' said Gudbrod Gudbrodsson, who always had an answer for everything.

Thorfinn Thorfinnson said, 'Then I come poorly out of the test, for my legs are shaking like those of a beggar stricken with palsy !'

But Harald and Grummoch merely flung back their matted heads and laughed, as though the flight of arrows was greatly to their taste. Then they turned and went up the beach, side by side, with their men behind them, never once looking back, or showing any fear whatever.

And when they were within ten paces of the thickly knotted line of red men, they halted.

There was an old man, heavily laden with feathers and

wearing copper bands the length of his two arms, which stuck out from holes in his long skin robe; and it was to this old man that Harald spoke the first words. He used the Innuit tongue, slowly and with care.

'Greetings,' he said. 'We are men of peace.'

For a long while the red man did not reply, but the younger ones behind him whispered and nudged each other. The vikings saw that every one had an arrow ready on his bowstring.

Once more Harald said, 'We are men of peace.'

Then the old man who wore the red feathers about his head slapped his chest, and said, in a tongue most like that of the Innuit, but different in some of its lilting, 'We Beothuk are great warriors. Are you great warriors?'

Harald saw then that this question had placed him in a cleft stick, for if he said that the Northmen were great warriors, then the red men might challenge them to fight without delay; and if he said that the Northmen were not great warriors, then the red men might kill them out of contempt. He thought quickly and then said, 'Only the Gods can answer that question. We fight other men when they invite us to do so. We sit about the fire with other men when they invite us, and do not fight them. That is all.'

The red men chattered among themselves, and one great fellow with a barrel chest strutted forward and bowed his plaited head before the man with the feather headdress, speaking to him rapidly with much waving of a great club studded along its edge with shark's teeth.

Grummoch whispered, 'That is the man we have to fear. If he is their champion, I beg you, Harald, to let me meet him. My axe, *Death Kiss*, is in need of a flesh-ing.'

Harald said, 'It shall be as you say; but we must wait and see.'

They saw the old chief nod his feathered head. Then the barrel-chested man, who had tribal scars across his broad face, began to address the red men, shouting hoarsely and waving his brawny arms, as though trying to work them to a fury.

At last he turned round and faced Harald.

In a high-pitched tone he said, 'You are dogs. We are men.'

Thorfinn Thorfinnson whispered, 'I knew that some-thing ill would come from our living so long in the dog-house among the Innuit. Even the red men can smell dog on us now.'

Gudbrod Gudbrodsson said, 'Lift up your jerkin and show them that you have not a curly tail, my friend.'

Thorfinn Thorfinnson whispered, 'I don't know about that. There is something shaking behind me, and it is not my sword-sheath.'

Then Grummoch stepped forward and flung his axe, *Death Kiss*, high into the blue air, so that it twisted and twirled as it went up and then came down. He caught it easily in his right hand, his lips set grim, his right foot forward, his great weight upon his left.

'Come forth, man,' he said, 'and let me show how this dog bites.'

The red men were silent then, and lowered their bows, as though anxious not to miss what might happen.

The barrel-chested warrior slapped his thighs, left and right, then began a little jigging dance upon the sand, as though to work up his courage. Then, almost without warning, he gave a high shriek and bounded to the spot where Grummoch waited.

The viking stood as still as a stone until the red man's blow came down, then thrust out his axe-shaft and caught the club so that many of the shark's teeth broke off and flew into the air.

Once again the angry red man struck, and once more the giant thrust out his axe-shaft, warding off the blow.

Now the red man stood uncertain for a moment, wondering how best to come at Grummoch; and while he stood so, Grummoch suddenly gave a deep bellowing cry, like that of a bull in the last extreme of fury, and leapt forward. The red man held up his already splintered club to stave off the axe-sweep, but Grummoch struck shrewdly that day. One blow he struck, and that blow sheared through the war-club as though it had been made of soft clay. One blow he struck, and that blow came near to shattering the proud chest of the redman warrior.

Save that, in the last inches, Grummoch turned his axeblade with a quick twist of the hand, so that the weapon struck with its flat and not with its edge.

The red man gave a groan, the breath knocked quite from him, and fell backwards, ploughing up the sand with the force of his fall, for he was a heavy man, and fell sprawling, his arms and legs spread like those of a star-fish.

Grummoch stepped forward grimly, as though he might be about to strike down once more at the dazed red man. Both vikings and red warriors were silent, their faces grim. The old chief bowed down his head, as though he

would not be willing to watch his champion shamed so. But no man raised a weapon to hurt Grummoch as he stood above the warrior.

Then, at the last moment, the giant bent and touched the red man lightly on the forehead with his axe-flat, and said for all to hear, 'The luck was with me. Thus I touch you in sign of axe-friendship now. Rise and be my brother.'

Thorfinn said quietly, 'That is easier said than done. The poor fellow's ribs will be too sore for him to get about unaided for a week, I reckon.'

And when the red man made an effort to rise, but could not, Grummoch bent again and picked him up as easily as though he were lifting a child, though the red man was bigger than most men of the Northlands.

And when he did this, the other red men waved their hatchets and began to shout, as though they had gained a victory, not a defeat.

Then the old chief came forward and said, 'This is my son, Wawasha. Though I love him, you must give him death if you so will, for by the laws of our people he may not accept life from any man. If you do not kill him, then expect no thanks from him ever. It is your choice.'

And Grummoch said, 'Wawasha is a brave warrior. I, Grummoch, man of the Northlands, love brave warriors and do not wish to kill them. Let Wawasha be my brother and also the brother of my oath-brother, Harald Sigurdson. I do not wish a red warrior to thank me for sparing him; I only wish that he shall become my brother and that our bravery shall go forward together.'

Then Wawasha, who had regained some of his breath, though his face was still deathly pale, smiled ruefully and said, 'Let it be so.'

And, as Grummoch and Harald and Wawasha made a little circle, each holding the other's hand in friendship, the Beothuk people began to shout and to dance on the sand where they stood, waving their feathered hatchets and nodding their black heads up and down like the heads of horses.

Gudbrod Gudbrodsson said, 'One brother is worth ten enemies.'

Jamsgar Havvarson said, 'Aye, but a brother at dawn may be an enemy at sunset.'

'Oh, go on with you,' said Thorfinn Thorfinnson. 'You are like an old Lappland butterwoman at a Spring Fair – full of strange omens, with a black cat on your head.'

Jamsgar Havvarson who was a simple soul felt on his head then, and said, 'I have no black cat on my head, only my hair.'

Gudbrod Gudbrodsson said, 'Hold tightly to it, friend, for if you can see what I see, these Beothuk seem fond of collecting other men's hair. Look at the scalps which hang from their belts.'

Jamsgar Havvarson said, 'I shall put my hat on then, for I have no wish to lose my hair, full of Innuit lice though it may be. I value my hair. It is very pretty when it is well combed and made into plaits. Indeed, along the fjord, there are women who say that they have never seen hair like it.'

Thorfinn Thorfinnson said, 'Indeed, they speak the truth, for it sticks out like the hay in a rick; it is coarse like that of a sow; and it is thin like that of an old donkey. In truth, friend, keep your hat on for if such a treasure were lost, its like would never be found again in all the Northland.'

Jamsgar nodded gravely. 'I shall do that, friend,' he said.

Then they followed the red men up the shore to a green place among the trees, from which the blue smoke was rising into the still air.

Chapter **12** *Beothuk*

The vikings found life among the Beothuk much to their liking, especially after their long stay in the ice-bound land of Innuit and their bitter journeys over the sea-crests.

The old chief, Gichita, allowed Harald and Grummoch to sit with him and his son, Wawasha, nearest the fire, and even gave them feather headdresses as a sign that they were accepted into the tribe as warriors. These were fur caps, into which hawk and eagle feathers were set at front and rear. The one which Grummoch wore was edged with small silver buttons which clinked as he moved. Harald's headdress had a band of white beads upon a broad blue cloth background.

When Gichita made the presentation of these head-dresses, he said, 'Great warriors should wear the signs of their fame.'

Gichita's young daughter, Neneoshaweg, taught the vikings how to dress their hair in Beothuk style, drawing it down at the back in a long tail and pulling it through a tube of bone, so that it stayed there when they ran through the thick woodland.

'This is less trouble than plaiting our hair, oath-brother,' said Grummoch to Harald. 'The only thing is that this tube of bone bounces between my shoulders when I move, and that is worrying. I keep turning round, thinking that someone has tapped me on the back.'

Harald answered, 'That is a thought which you can cease to worry over. If ever you are tapped between the shoulderblades here, there will be little point in turning round. The damage will be done by then!'

But in spite of this grim jest, life among the Beothuk was pleasant for a while. The vikings made presents to Gichita of iron swords and axes, which had belonged to the men who were lost on that perilous trip from Iceland to Greenland; and in return Gichita gave them feathered hatchets of stone and elk-bone, and also hunting knives, beaten from copper and from cold iron, their blades set in the horn of great stags or elks.

And soon the vikings took to wearing the warrior-paint across their faces, in broad bands, sometimes blue from a woodland plant, and sometimes yellow, made from a clay which the Beothuk dug from a damp glade near the settlement.

Gudbrod Gudbrodsson said one day, 'This face-covering becomes you well, Thorfinn Thorfinnson.'

Thorfinn bowed his head solemnly, after the manner of the Beothuk. 'I am pleased to hear you say that, my friend,' he answered.

Gudbrod nodded. 'Aye,' he said, 'it becomes you well because it covers your ugliness so that you seem less like an ape from Jebel Tarik and more like a man, though a very strange man at that!'

Thorfinn gave a snort and walked away to where the musicians were playing on their drums and bone flutes and one-stringed harps.

And there, in the glade, to the monotonous rhythms, Grummoch danced the Bear Dance, which he had once learned in Lappland, bending his great body and shuffling one foot after the other, his thick arms hanging down before him.

This pleased the Beothuk, who knew well enough what the dance symbolized; and soon they, too, were imitating him, for this dance was greatly to their taste.

The vikings were welcome in other ways, for they were great tellers of stories about the evening fires and before they went to lie down in their hide sleeping-bags under the skin awnings in the glade.

The story which Harald told was most admired by all, and he was asked to tell it again, and again, until the Beothuk knew every word of it.

'Once, years ago,' he began, 'the great goddess Freya had two sons – one, Balder the Handsome, the other Hoder the Blind. Fine was it to see Balder riding his white horse through the skies,' (here he had to stop and explain what a horse was, for the Beothuk had never seen one) 'and sad was it to watch poor Hoder stumbling among the forest roots, helpless. For Balder was a man among men, much like Wawasha here, while Hoder was of little use save to eat meat by the warm fire and to snuggle into his sheep-skin bed at night.'

When Harald spoke these words, a strange silence fell upon the listening Beothuk, who all looked towards a pale youth sitting at the back of the circle.

'Freya was so pleased with her warrior son,' Harald went on, 'that during one Spring feasting she called upon birds, beasts, and trees of the woodland to swear a great oath never to harm Balder. She even made the thunder-clouds and the rushing waters swear this oath, too, which they did willingly, for Balder was such a favourite in the Northern world.

'And when earth, water, fire and iron had sworn never to hurt Balder, Odin thought it was time for the feast-jesting to begin, and called upon all the warriors and champions to hew or to shoot at him, to prove whether the oaths had been sworn well. And they had, for swords, axes and arrows fell harmless from the young viking's body, and he smiled as the champions thrust at him with spears, for they slid away from him, though he wore no armour.

'It was while this feasting was going on, the horn-cup passing from hand to hand, that Loki the Mischief-maker came to Freya and asked if there was nothing in the whole wide world that could hurt this splendid fellow. And Freya, drinking with the men, answered carelessly that there was one thing – a plant called the mistletoe, which grew eastwards of the hall of Valhalla, and was too weak and too young to be the cause of any fear.

'So that night Loki put on his dark cloak and crept out of the noisy hall, and went to the grove where the mistletoe grew. And there he cut down a twig of the plant and shaped it into a little javelin with his sharp knife, *Evil-doer*. Then he returned, the twig hidden beneath his dark cloak, and went to Balder's brother, Hoder, who stood silently among the shouters, at the edge of the circle.

' "Why do you not join in the merrymaking, Hoder?" asked Loki.

' "Because I cannot see where my brother stands, and because I have no weapon with which to strike at him," answered the blind one.

'Loki said, "Such things are not beyond the wit of man

or god to set right. Let me lead you forward through the hall and set you close to Balder, so that you may throw this stick at him, in token that you too have tested him. For it ill becomes a brother to hang back at a time like this, when everyone, even the kitchen-thralls, have honoured him by striking at his weapon-proof body."

'So blind Hoder let Loki take him to a spot before the laughing Balder, and set the mistletoe spear in his weak hand, and guided his hand, so that the shaft flew towards Balder's heart.

'All men gave way when Hoder made his cast, for he was of the kingly blood and was not to be denied anything.

'But when the little shaft struck Balder, it sank deep into his heart, and the handsome warrior-god fell forward on his face, trying to drag out the strange weapon which had brought his death upon him. But it had bitten too shrewdly, and Balder died on the floor of the feast-hall with his friends weeping over him.

'Loki slid quickly away into the darkness. No man blamed Hoder, for it was seen what a trick had been played upon him by Loki. So Balder's brief hour of triumph was over.

'Then, among weeping, the shield-men carried Balder's body down to the fjord and laid it aboard his longship, *Ringhorn*, the hugest of all ships ever built along the fjords. And with him on the funeral pile lay Nanna, his wife, who had died of grief that night. And at his feet lay Balder's great white stallion, Reksgor, with all his golden trappings.

'And so, at last, after some difficulties, the longship was sent blazing across the fjord, where at last it sank.

Both gods and men wept sorely, feeling that something had gone from their lives.'

When Harald had finished, there was a great silence about the camp-fire of the Beothuk, for this tale moved them every bit as much as it moved the listening vikings, many of whom let the salt tears fall upon their chests without shame.

To lighten this silence, Grummoch said, 'Gichita, this is an old tale. Do not weep. You have a son every bit as handsome and as warrior-like as Balder. Wawasha is such a one.'

Then Gichita rose and pointed to the pale-faced youth who sat at the edge of the fire-circle.

'Yes,' he said, 'and I have, also, a son who greatly resembles poor Hoder, except that his hands and not his eyes are useless. Come forth, Heome, and let our stranger-brothers see your hands.'

The braves about the fire moved back, so that Heome might obey his father and stand before Harald and Grummoch. This he did only after his father, Gichita, had spoken three times, and then with a bad grace, which showed in the expression on his pale face.

Standing in the firelight, under the low spruce boughs, he said bitterly, 'Here are my hands, white strangers. Feast your pale eyes upon them and laugh in your hearts. A brown bear of the forest tore them when I was but a lad. Look on them and smile!'

He held out his wasted arms and the vikings saw that the hands were puckered and useless.

Gichita said with bowed head, 'This happened when Heome was in his twelfth year, at the time when the boys are initiated as braves. It is my sadness that Heome failed in his testing-time.'

Harald was about to find something to say which might give pleasure to the young man, but before his tongue could move, Heome gave a bitter laugh and said for all the warriors to hear, 'You sent me to the woods, my father. You commanded me to do that which has cost me my hands. On you rests the blame! On you rests the wretchedness of my crippled hands!'

Gichita bowed his head and covered his fierce old face in the blanket of buffalo-hide. But Wawasha, the great warrior, leaped up in the firelight, with the red glow upon his copper arm-bands and in the feathers on his head, and reached out his hands towards Heome.

'Brother,' he said, 'speak no more in that manner. Our father is old and should not be so tormented. He sent you to the woods because that is the custom of our people, not because he wished you harm. You are the flesh of his flesh; he would not wish that flesh to be hurt, brother!'

Heome turned in the firelight and spat in his brother's face. The gathered braves drew in their breath.

Heome said, 'Since I was twelve the women have fed me with bone spoons, and morsels in their fingers. Is that a life for a man? You tell me not to hurt my father; I tell you that I hate my father, for what he has done to me. I tell you that Gichita has lost my love.'

Then Heome began to weep, and the sound of his weeping in that twilit forest was worse than the sound of his anger, for it was the sound of a damned creature who had lost all hope and had nothing to live for.

Even the birds of the forest took up his weeping cry and echoed it along the avenues and glades, and for a while all the wild woodland was astir with the deep sadness of this red man's bitterness.

Harald rose and, thinking of his own wounded sons, said, 'All men have their sufferings.'

But he got no further, for Heome swung round upon him and said, 'Be quiet, dog, when your betters speak! One day I will see you burned in the slow fires for a meddling hound!'

And then he turned and strode away into the darkness beyond the firelight. The braves drew away so he might pass by unhindered.

Then Wawasha said, 'That is my only brother, whom I love more than I love my own right hand, and who hates me.'

And the old man, Gichita, said, 'I would suffer my own old hands to be smitten from me, if Heome could have back the use of his.'

After that, the singing and dancing, the story-telling, were over, for this quarrel about the fire cast a gloom upon all who were there.

In their own tent, Harald said to Grummoch, 'One day, Loki will come and teach crippled Hoder how to kill his brother Balder.'

Grummoch nodded. 'That thought ran in my own mind, too,' he said. 'Yet what can we do to prevent such a thing? We are strangers here, and a stranger does well to stay outside the door when his hosts quarrel within.'

Harald answered, 'Perhaps I did ill to tell that old Norse tale by the fire this evening.'

But Grummoch shook his head.

'The damage had been done long years before we sailed from Norway, oath-brother,' he said. 'You cannot blame yourself for Heome's misery.'

Harald thought for a while, then nodded his head, meaning that Grummoch was right.

'Yet,' he said, 'if the chance comes, I will see to it that Heome is accepted by his tribesfolk as a warrior. Then perhaps his thoughts of vengeance may be turned aside.'

That chance came sooner than Harald, or anyone else, expected.

Chapter 14 *Grey Wolf*

The hunters ran through the forest, silently as shadows. The vikings, who ran in a separate party, led by Harald, made rather more noise, not being used to this sort of thing.

From ahead of them, the vikings heard that the Beothuk had sighted their quarry by the high owl-cries which this folk made when excited.

Gudbrod Gudbrodsson said, 'When our folks see their enemy, they do not hoot like a flight of night-birds. They go in and finish him, silently.'

Thorfinn Thorfinnson said, 'That is because we are a modest folk, and brought up not to boast of our deeds. My uncle, Svend Threeswords, from under the hill near Gulpjefjord, once killed fifteen Danes in the night, as they slept in the heather, with one little knife. He wiped it and went home for his porridge and never a word did he say to my Aunt Besje, until she asked about the stains upon his arms. Then he said he had been picking black-berries. Another time he hung on a frayed rope above a deep gorge, when he was gathering samphire, for four-teen hours, and at the end of it, when a shepherd came and saw him and offered to drag him up, said, "Please yourself, fellow, I am prepared to go on dangling here until tomorrow. It is no effort when once one has got the hang of it." He was a modest man, you understand?'

Jamsgar Havvarson said, in his simple way, 'Yes, it

is true that we Northmen are anxious to avoid all praise. When my father sailed into Frankland and burned eight churches of the Whitechrist, the Pope offered him great reward for acting so valiantly, and promised him bed and board for life in the stoutest jail in Rome, if my father ever visited that city. But he did not go to claim his lifetime's lodgings. Other men would have jumped at the chance, but my father, who was a simple fellow, chose to stay at home with his goat Nessi and his four cows, whose names I now forget, rather than have his fame bruited abroad in Rome.'

'Indeed,' said Thorfinn, nudging Gudbrod, 'we are a modest folk. Let us hope that our modesty is well repaid by the gods.'

It was while they were thus talking and running that Harald almost stumbled over Heome, who lay under a juniper bush, exhausted at trying to keep up with the other Beothuk hunters.

Grummoch picked the young fellow up and slung him over his shoulder.

'Come, friend,' he said, 'you may not be able to kill a bear, but there is no reason why you should be left behind if there is anything to see.'

After a while, Heome tried to kick at Grummoch, in his anger at being so shamed, but the giant affected not to notice this display of temper, and so they went on. At last Heome made no further effort to resist.

And towards mid-day, when the sounds of the Beothuk had died away in the distance, the vikings came to a glade in which was a heap of stone slabs, almost overgrown by lichen and creeping plants. In that heap was a doorway, so that it looked like a little house.

Harald went forward to look into the doorway, but drew back as though he had been slapped across the face. Then all who were close by smelled the bitter scent of wolf.

Harald called out, 'There are two grown wolves in this lair. One is a dog-wolf, the other is a she-wolf with a litter of cubs.'

He had scarcely given this news when the great grey dog-wolf swept through the opening, his tail swirling in anger, and stood before the door, as though to guard it. All men noticed how strong in the jaw he seemed and how long in the teeth.

Gudbrod said, 'I had rather tackle that one with an axe than with a skillet-spoon, the weapon which my grand-mother used against the English when they came to visit up the fjord one Spring.'

Thorfinn said, 'This is the grandfather of all wolves. I have seen nothing like him in the Northland.'

Harald would have backed away, respecting the dog-wolf's right to protect his wife and children, but the great grey creature suddenly gave a low growl and flung himself at the viking, who stood not more than three paces away.

Harald saw the beast springing and knew that it would be foolish and also cowardly to try to avoid him. Therefore, he drew his hunting-knife and, leaning over so that the wild creature should not strike him in head or chest, held the keen blade in such a way that the grey wolf swept along it in the course of his flight through the air.

And when the wolf landed, howling with mortal agony, Harald turned on him and, apologizing, struck him just behind the skull, so that his end should be swift. The great grey wolf lay still, silent now, and giving forth only the slightest tremor of the hind-legs.

Jamsgar Havvarson said reflectively, 'No blow was struck more shrewdly, not even among the Lapps, who are very able with the small knife. If I were a king, Sigurdson here should have a gold arm-ring for this brave deed.'

Thorfinn Thorfinnson said, 'If you were a king, no one would have a gold ring but you, and that you would keep in an oak chest buried in the ground, while you went in rags. I know your sort of king.'

But before this wrangling could go further, Grummoch went forward and whispered in Harald's ear. Harald nodded, as though in agreement.

Then he turned and spoke to Heome, who now stood trembling at the edge of the glade.

'Heome, son of Gichita,' he said, 'all the world knows that you are a brave fellow, only prevented by your wounded hands from showing your valour. To prove this valour to your folk, I give you this wolf. We can say that you grappled with it, and had it nigh dead, when one of my men ran forward and gave it the end-stroke. How would that please you?'

For a while, Heome's dark eyes went from Harald to the wolf and back. Then he said, his pale lips twitching, 'Such a deed would make my people respect me at last. They would accept me as a man for killing a wolf bare-handed. But what of these white men here – would they not speak of the wolf-killing and let fall the secret?'

Harald said, 'I promise you, there is no fear of that. These men are my friends and followers, who have sailed with me through many bitter storms, over many salt seas. They would not betray our secret; would you, vikings?'

The vikings, standing in the glade, shook their axes and promised never to speak of this affair again.

And so the party turned back, bearing the dead dog-wolf. Grummoch carried it, for it was full-grown and heavy, until they came within sight of Gichita's tepee, and then he passed it to Heome, who struggled along with his load to his father's skin house.

And there he laid it down before the old chief, and explained how he came to kill the fierce beast. The vikings stood behind him, their arms folded, nodding at every word.

At first Gichita looked doubtful but when he saw that Harald and Grummoch were nodding, too, he called the elders of the Beothuk Council, and solemnly they declared that Heome was now a brave and a full man.

The squaws skinned the wolf and made a head-covering for Heome from the pelt. His new name was 'Wolf-slayer'.

When Wawasha returned, carrying deer upon a pole, he saw Heome strutting about among the squaws in his new finery, and asked what had happened. And when Harald told him that Heome had now proved himself a warrior, Wawasha ran to his brother and clasped him in his arms, almost weeping with pleasure that this should be so.

But the vikings observed that Heome shrugged off his brother's embraces, his lips curling proudly, so that Wawasha was somewhat hurt.

Grummoch said in a whisper, 'Perhaps we have not done as well as we thought, oath-brother.'

Harald said thoughtfully, 'Perhaps. But that rests with the gods. We have sworn to keep the secret, and from now on the incident is closed.'

But there were many among the vikings during that feast-night who regretted that they had taken the oath in the glade that day, for they could not abide a proud coward, being warriors themselves.

Now the Spring was at its height, and all the trees were full and green. Young deer and foxes ran in abundance through the glades. Birds nested in every tree. Hawk and eagle hovered in the blue sky, seeking prey for their young.

And, at last, Gichita called his folk together and said, 'Now is the time when we leave our cooking-place in the forest and move to the great plains where there is meat and hide enough to feed all the world and to clothe them through the winter. Make ready, for this is the journey-season and we must not miss the fine weather, if we wish our canoes to sail smoothly through the waters of river and lake.'

During the next two days, the braves patched and greased their long skin canoes, and carried them down to the water. There they loaded them with all that would be needed for the Spring journey – meal and dried meat, the carcasses of young deer, wine-skins of buffalo-hide, and all the weapons of the chase.

Long Snake still lay at anchor by the shore, and the vikings prepared her, too, for the long voyage inland, little knowing what they were to find there.

On the day before they were due to sail, Wawasha came aboard and said, 'Gichita, my father, will lead this sailing, and the new warrior, Heome, will sit in the canoe with him to guide the folk. Let me sail with you, stranger-

brothers, in this great canoe of wood. It is something I have wished to do ever since I saw you come to the shore.'

Harald took him by his strong brown hand and said, 'Willingly, Wawasha. I would wish for nothing else. You are the first red viking!'

Then all the Northmen began to laugh, and Gudbrod Gudbrodsson gave Wawasha an iron helmet set with bull's horns, and decorated at the front with a strip of copper inlaid with red garnets.

This gift pleased Wawasha greatly, and he swore that he would always wear it, heavy though it was, as a sign of their brotherhood.

And when the hunting-party set off, Wawasha stood in the prow of *Long Snake*, with Harald and Grummoch, looking so proud that the vikings swore they had never seen a better man, no, not even along the fjords back in Northland.

'If only he carried a proper axe of iron, instead of that little woodpecker!' said Thorfinn.

Gudbrod said, 'Have no fears, that little woodpecker could do as much damage as your great wood-cleaver! Think, my clever friend, Wawasha has only to go Pick! Pick! and a man is no more. Whereas you have to swing your lump of iron set on a tree-trunk twice round your head before you can strike a blow – and then you are exhausted!'

Thorfinn said, 'Why, I do declare, you are more than half a red man yourself by now. Why do you not put on a hide shirt with fringes at the edge?'

Gudbrod said, 'I have been thinking that myself, friend. They are very warm, and are much more serviceable than the old woollen jerkin I am wearing at the moment.'

Thorfinn said, 'Oh, go and paint your face, you savage!'

But in his heart, Thorfinn also admired the Beothuk, and especially Wawasha, who would one day be a great war-leader as fine as any man of the Northland.

Only two things bothered the mind of Harald Sigurdson; one was the dream that now came to him almost every night, of his wife and two sons, who stood on a hilltop above the fjord, holding out their hands to him and asking with their eyes when he would come back to their village. The other was the behaviour of the new warrior, Heome, who lost no opportunity of pointing out his great prowess to all he met.

On the first day of the sailing towards the west, Harald drew Grummoch aside into the sheltered place at the stern of the longship and said, 'Grummoch, there are two questions I wish to ask you, old axe-friend.'

Grummoch scratched his tawny head and said, 'Ask on, Harald my oath-brother; provided that you do not want to know where winds come from, or what makes the moon round like a plate. I do not know the answers to those questions, I will be frank with you. Though I fancy I could answer you almost any other question!'

For a jest, Harald almost asked him where the tides started, but he did not, for he was at heart serious now. He asked instead, 'Would it not be wiser for us to turn our ship round and sail towards the rising sun, towards our homes, and not towards the sinking sun?'

Grummoch said, 'That also had been in my mind, for we have been a long time from our homes. But consider — we are fewer than we were when we set out from the fjord. Until we can persuade some of the Beothuk to sail with us, we would make a poor showing back across the broad waters. Besides, it is the duty of every Northman who comes as far as this to take back treasure to his village, and we have not found treasure yet. It is my hope that if we go with the Beothuk inland, we may chance upon gold or silver, or precious stones, which can be carried easily in *Long Snake*. Then we should return home with the knowledge that the long voyage had not been wasted. Does that answer your first question, friend?'

Harald nodded, yet in his heart was still the great yearning to set eyes once again upon his dear wife, Asa Thornsdaughter, and upon his two sons, Svend and Jaroslav.

'What is your second question, Harald?' asked Grummoch, scratching his side idly, as though he were a great prophet, to whom the answering of questions came as easily as swatting flies.

Harald said, 'I am worried in my mind about Heome. He was once weak and despised among his folk, because of his powerless hands; but we have given him manhood, hoping to give him pride in himself. Yet all that has happened is that he has gained contempt for all. Now he lords it above the warriors, and even speaks to his warrior brother, Wawasha, as though he is a dog beneath him. One day, I fear, he will betray his brother and perhaps try to kill him, so that he, Heome, will become chief of the Beothuk when Gichita dies. Moreover, it is in my mind that Heome will try to do away with us, for we know his secret, having made him what he is now.'

Grummoch yawned and said, 'Heome is still nothing more than a gnat that bites, such as these which follow the ship. They are irritating, but nothing more. When one wishes to be rid of them, it is an easy matter to waft them away. And if one settles on a man's arm and tries to bite, it is an easy matter to slap them into nothingness with one pat of the hand. So it is with Heome. He calls himself Heome the Wolf; I call him Heome the Gnat. If Heome the Gnat offends me, I shall pat him with my hand, and he will be nothing but a memory.'

Harald nodded, thoughtfully. 'Brave words, friend,' he answered. 'But brave words are not always wise words. I have often watched the face of Heome, and have seen in it a strange sort of power, as though when the time came, he might well be a man to reckon with, and not a mere gnat. We must not underestimate him, Grummoch. He could do us an injury.'

Grummoch began to hum a tuneless little ditty, then he said, 'We will take that chance when it comes, Harald. When I think of the men I put paid to in Ireland, in the

time of King MacMiorog, I laugh at the thought of deal-
ing with little Heome.'

Harald replied, 'The men you met, years ago when
you were young and lusty, were simple warriors, whose
only strength was in their axe or their sword. Once you
had overcome axe and sword, those men were finished.
But Heome is not an axeman or a swordman; he has no
hands to hold such simple weapons. His weapon is in his
mind, and that is the craftiest weapon of all – for it will
attack in unsuspected ways, in a bear-pit, a falling tree,
an avalanche, a hole in the bottom of a boat, poison in a
drinking-cup, a cord round the neck while one is sleeping.'

Grummoch answered, 'We are all in the hands of Odin,
oath-brother. What will come, will come; and there is no
doing anything about it. Why, you might as well worry
about that misty Shield-maiden who came to you when
we left Haakon's man, Havlock Ingolfson, on the skerry
to drown.'

Harald answered sadly, 'You speak truer than you
know, friend! I *do* worry about her, every other day. I
am not a child to be put off with sweet words; I know
that I did wrong that night in leaving the poor wretch
to drown on the lonely skerry, and I know that Odin
will punish me for it, in one way or another, before he
has done with me. It may even be that he has already
chosen Heome the Gnat to be my death-giver.'

Grummoch laughed aloud at this, and made Harald
drink a horn of red berry juice, to put him in a better
frame of mind.

But though this remedy worked for an hour, it did not
last the day out, and towards evening he was sad again.

He would not even join the other vikings at axe-throwing, a pastime which whiled away the tedious hours for them.

They set up a cord, no thicker than a man's small finger and drawn tight between two sticks. Then they went back ten paces and aimed their axes at it, trying to cut the cord in the centre. Harald was usually the first to do this; but now he shrugged his friends away when they asked him to join them.

Gudbrod Gudbrodsson said, 'Friend Harald is in a black mood tonight.'

Jamsgar Havvarson said, 'I think he has a stomach-ache which is bothering him. That is the only thing I know which can make a man look so thoughtful.'

They crossed a narrow stretch of water on the first two days, and then camped for a night under beetling mountains, with the wolves howling above them as the moon rose, pale and full.

This was a green land, but lonely.

'Who lives here?' asked Harald of Wawasha.

Wawasha spread his great hands and shrugged his brown shoulders.

'Few men,' he said. 'Tribes who do not give themselves names, but hunt only in small parties. They are not men like us; they wear fur about them, like bears, and come from far far North. The Moon is their Goddess and they feed rather on the fat than on the flesh of the creatures they kill. They are not men to be afraid of, for when they see us coming with our feathers and our axes, they run away into the forests.'

Grummoch said, 'Are there any men you are afraid of, Wawasha?'

Wawasha said, 'A Beothuk brave is afraid of no man, giant. But there are some men we treat with caution; men such as the Algonkin, who live a moon's distance up the great river we shall enter before long. They are fierce warriors, and there are many of them. They do not love the Beothuk, because once, many generations ago, some of our young men landed on their shore and chopped down their sacred tree. not knowing what they did, but only wishing to build a shelter for themselves against the storms that come on towards the close of the hunting season, when we make our way back to our own cooking-place.'

Harald asked, 'What of the Algonkin? Do they come out to fight with you, friend?'

Wawasha nodded. 'Some years they lie waiting for us to come up the great river; then there is bloodshed. But some years they stand on the shore and watch us go past, hoping that the river will kill us – for there are many hazards there, rapids, waterfalls, rocks and land-slides.'

Grummoch asked, 'Why then do you go every year inland, when there is food enough to be got from your own forests?'

Wawasha said, 'We go for many reasons. First, because the great God, Gichguma, commanded us to go, at the beginning of the world; secondly, because our tribe have always gone, just as most other tribes have gone; and lastly because we must visit the great quarries beside the lake, where the sacred stone is dug out of the ground. Nowhere in all the world can this sacred stone be found, but in this place. Without it, we could not make our peace-pipes or the necklaces which protect us from thunder and lightning.'

He put his hand within his light robe and drew out a long necklace of red stone. Each bead was carved in the shape of a man's head, and was threaded on a thin string of buckskin.

Harald handled this necklace gently. 'This stone is hard, Wawasha,' he said. 'How could it be made into such fine shapes, then?'

Wawasha drew the necklace away from the viking's fingers, quietly, as though it might lose its magic if it were handled too long by another.

'When it is first dug,' he said, 'it is as soft as clay; and it is then that we shape it with our knives. But later it grows hard and keeps its shape, as you have felt. This necklace was made by the father of my father's father, and that was many lives ago. It is still unbroken, as you see. It is very strong medicine, too, for not one who has worn it was ever harmed by thunder or lightning.'

Grummoch said, 'I must have one of those, then Thor can do his worst!'

Thorfinn Thorfinnson, who had been listening, said, 'It is foolish to speak so, Grummoch Giant. Thor may well be listening, and may decide to strike you down before you can dig such a necklace. Then where would you be?'

The giant shrugged his massive shoulders. 'Burnt to crackling under a tree, I expect,' he said. 'What worry is that to you, Thorfinn Thorfinnson?'

The other said, 'It is a great worry, for I might be standing beside you, and then I, too, would be burned to a crackling under a tree.'

Gudbrod Gudbrodsson said, 'Then you would be cooked in good company. That would be better than being cooked with Jamsgar Havvarson, who is a skinny man and would not cook well.'

Wawasha listened to the vikings as they wrangled, but he had learned now that this was their manner, and that ill seldom came from such arguments, unless the vikings had been drinking berry-juice, or held axes in their hands when the discussion started. But this night, none of them held axes, and few of them had had more than a sip of the red juice from the stone gourds.

The next day they started before dawn, and made their way along the shore, the braves in the canoes paddling slowly, in their accustomed manner, at a pace which they could keep up all day without resting, if they needed to do so.

The longship sailed among them, an east wind in her great sail, like a mother goose among her many goslings, for in truth the canoes of the Beothuk floated as thick as seeds upon the broad waters.

Chapter 17 *Algonkin*

The new moon had come and gone when *Long Snake* and the many Beothuk canoes left the broad waters, and ran into the narrow mouth of the river. Now the voyagers could see the shore on either side, not more than three bowshots away.

It was growing dusk when Wawasha first sniffed the air, like a questing hound, and then whispered, 'I smell danger, friends.'

The red men in the canoes were holding up their heads as Wawasha had done, and now among them passed a slight stirring, a shimmering of concern. The canoes seemed to bunch together, rubbing side by side, as though they were living creatures, deer perhaps, who had caught the sudden acrid whiff of wolf-scent.

Harald whispered, 'Are they Algonkin, Wawasha?'

The Beothuk warrior nodded. 'Algonkin and Abnaki, my nose tells me. I had not thought to smell Algonkin yet awhile; and most years the Abnaki folk move towards the coast, not inland. To smell them both together is bad. Abnaki alone mean little harm, but when they are with others they grow brave and dream that they are a great people once again.'

Now Gichita's canoe pulled alongside *Long Snake*, and the old chief whispered hoarsely to his son, 'I have seen lights on both sides of the river, Wawasha. The men in the forests there are waiting for us, and care not if we see their fires. That means they are strong. What do you counsel, my son? are we to go forward, or to turn back and make the journey later in the year, when these tribes have moved away?'

Wawasha said, 'The Beothuk folk have never yet turned back from Algonkin, still less from Abnaki, who are eaters of squirrels and drinkers of muddy water! We have our white brothers with us now, and that should make us a match for such warriors as lie in wait for us tonight. I counsel you, father, to let the canoes containing the squaws and the young children draw behind *Long Snake*, and we will go forward like true warriors.'

Heome sat in the prow of his father's canoe, his hands shaking, his pale lips trembling.

'Let us go back, father,' he said, his voice thin and afraid. 'My brother, Wawasha, thinks only of the glory he will gain, perhaps. But I think of our people. What will it profit us, even though Wawasha hangs ten scalps in his tent, if the pick of our warriors are left dead upon these shores?'

Gichita did not turn to answer his younger son, but still gazed up into Wawasha's face, as though waiting for his final word.

Now the warriors swung their canoes alongside that of their chief, waiting tensely for the words which were to be spoken.

Wawasha said, 'Never in my life have I turned away from battle. Nor shall I turn away tonight. If you, my father, listen to Heome's words and go back down the river, I shall still go forward with the white warriors in

Long Snake, for this quarrel with the Algonkin must have an ending. If we run away from them now, never again shall we be allowed to pass on up the river to dig the sacred stone. All the folk of woodland and plains will speak of us with laughter and call us dogs and eaters of carrion. That is my answer!'

Gichita bowed his head and said, 'So be it, my son. That is the answer I expected you to make, and the answer I wanted to hear.'

But Heome gave a low cry, like that of a woman who is suddenly afraid, and flung himself down in the canoe, covering his head with his buffalo robe.

Gudbrod Gudbrodsson said quietly, 'How can such a father have such a son? I am baffled by the ways of Odin Manmaker.'

Thorfinn Thorfinnson said, 'Odin Manmaker made thee and me; but he cannot be blamed for red men. They are the children of some other god.'

Darkness had fallen and the moon stood like a silver sickle in the night sky, casting down little light. All about him, Harald Sigurdson heard the small sounds of men unwrapping arrows, or stringing bows, drawing knives from sheaths, feeling for war-axes. The canoes lay still upon the darkly gleaming waters for a while, the men in them as nervous as hounds before the hunt.

Then Gichita whispered, 'Onward! May Thunder-voice bring us victory!'

Grummoch muttered, 'I'll set my trust in axe *Death Kiss*! This Thunder-voice may not come when I call him — but I know where *Death Kiss* is!'

Harald Sigurdson said, 'I have sword *Peace-giver* in my right hand, so I am content. When the blow-trading begins, brother, see that we stand back to back, then we shall know that the odds are fair ones, even if these Algonkin come at us ten to one!'

And all along the deck of *Long Snake* vikings spoke so to their war-brothers, in the old manner, arranging how they would meet their enemies. Thorfinn stood with Gudbrod; Jamsgar stood with a tall youth from Jomsberg, named Knud Ulfson. This youth was fond of needlework, and wore his yellow hair in four thick plaits, bound round with copper wire.

Yet no one in *Long Snake* thought it wise to offend him, for he came of a family of fifteen berserks, and had himself taken the heads of three Saxons before he was fourteen.

Then Gichita hooted like a night-owl, and the canoes swept on.

For a while nothing happened, and there were those on the dark water that night who began to think that this was a false alarm, when suddenly from either side of them in the thick woodlands, rose the war-yells of the Algonkin, like the yapping of foxes in wintertime; and then came the bear-grunts which were the battle-cries of the Abnaki.

For a moment or two the air seemed to murmur with arrows. Harald felt a shaft pass under his right arm, and then heard it slap against the oaken side of *Long Snake*.

'That was a close call,' he muttered to Grummoch, who was humming a little tune which always came to his lips when there was fighting to be had.

'Aye,' said the giant, shuffling his great shoulders, 'and doubtless there will be others before this night is out!'

Then from all about them, the vikings heard the horrible death chant of the Algonkin:

'Where is my enemy? Where is my enemy?
   Catch him quick!
Where is my enemy? Where is my enemy?
   Catch him quick!
Chop off his hands! Chop off his head!
Where is my enemy? Where is my enemy?
   Catch him quick!'

Thorfinn Thorfinnson said, 'It ill becomes a stranger in these parts, like myself, to speak harshly of the local skalds, but I have it in my mind that this song of theirs would better become children at a hopping-game than grown men about the noble business of battle. When this affair is over and we have a little leisure to think of gentle things, I shall set my mind to making a decent battle song that we may use when such occasions arise.'

But Thorfinn Thorfinnson never carried out his promise, for suddenly the *Long Snake* echoed with the swift passing of slippered feet and into every man's nostrils came the smell of the rancid bear-fat with which the red men coated their bodies before an affray, so that their enemies might not gain a fast grip about them.

Thorfinn was the first to fall, with a lance-point between his shoulder-blades. Yet even so he twisted and with his last strength took with him the Algonkin who had made the deadly thrust.

After which, Gudbrod, his henchman, set his back against the mast and had enough to worry about thereafter.

Harald and Grummoch, their eyes now grown used to the dusk, began their terrible battle-laugh. They were too big to escape the notice of the red men who swarmed upon the decks, and therefore they decided to go down into the red pit like the warriors they were.

That laughter echoed over the churned waters of the river, and struck terror into many hearts that night.

Harald struck out with *Peace-giver*.

'One !' he said, laughing.

Grummoch struck out with *Death Kiss*.

'One,' he said, laughing.

A sly lithe shape twisted under Harald's arm. The viking shortened his weapon and drove it upwards as the tomahawk bit. He heard a deep and gurgling groan.

'Two and a scratch,' he said, changing his sword to his left hand.

Grummoch swept *Death Kiss* in a wide scything motion about him, for the black shadows were thick on his side. Only he knew how many times that sharp edge took its meal; yet it was for every man to hear the cries which followed.

'Three and no scratch !' he said grimly, and began to laugh as though he owned the skies.

Harald said, 'Go slower. I cannot keep up with you, oath-brother ! It is not fair !'

Then they both began to laugh as though they rode with the Valkyries across the darkened North sky under the stars.

Behind them Jamsgar Havvarson felt his sword carried away from him when he had buried it deep, and now he fought on with bare hands, warding off blows with his forearms and then grappling and throttling. At his feet lay four braves of the Abnaki, before a shrewd thrust of the knife laid him low.

He said with his last breath, 'Knud Ulfson, I must be a little out of practice. If I do not wake from this sleep, go to my wife and daughters beside the fjord and give them my regards.'

Then he died, and Knud Ulfson felt the great pulse begin to beat in his temple like a war-drum. This was a sign he knew, but always forgot, once it started. It was the berserk sign.

While Grummoch smashed down with the back-point of his axe and called out, 'Eight!', and Harald, hardly able to stand now, replied with 'Six!', Knud Ulfson began the song which his family had always sung on occasions like this; for they were all berserks:

> 'Alas, my friend has gone away!
> Away from the field and the fjord!
> He leaves kine and kin,
> Bread and board,
> He leaves his wine-cup empty upon the bench.
> Just it is only that I go
> To where he is, and visit him!
> But to get there I must pass
> Through a dark low doorway
> Guarded by trolls!
> No troll shall prevent Knud Ulfson
> From visiting his friend!
> So, go you, troll!
> Go you, troll!
> Go, troll!
> To death!'

He marked the beat of his song with great blows, and at each blow a red man fell back, sometimes silent, sometimes howling, until at last none came near Knud Ulfson, for he had built about himself a barricade of Algonkin and Abnaki.

Grummoch called out, 'Twelve. But this axe-edge is not now what it was, and some blows have to be struck twice! I must sharpen it in the morning. This will never do!'

Harald leaned hard against him, his chest and arms streaming with the hot red wine of war.

'Nine,' he said, and sank to the deck.

Grummoch felt him go, and stepped back so that he straddled him, swinging *Death Kiss*.

In the canoe below *Long Snake*, Wawasha straddled his old father in the same way. Heome lay huddled beneath a heap of blankets, hardly daring to breathe lest he be discovered.

And so at last those who were left of the attackers scrambled for their lives over the side of the longship and fell into the water when they could not see their canoes, and paddled as quickly as their wounds would let them towards the wooded shores.

No longer did they yap like winter foxes, or grunt like forest bears. All their breath was needed for the paddles.

And when they had gone, Wawasha called up to the longship, 'Let us follow them, now, my friends, and finish this affair as it should be finished, by burning their boats and their villages. They must have cause to remember us for ever!'

But Grummoch, who did not know yet how badly his oath-brother was hurt, said back, 'Go you, with your braves, and light the little fires yourselves. It would ill become a Northman to sail with his decks uncleared and we have much tidying up to do. But call for us if you are hard pressed and we will come then.'

Wawasha said no more, but set off with all the war-boats he could gather. And shortly the woodland shores on either side of the river glowed with flame.

Wawasha lost no men in that village-burning, for the Algonkin and the Abnaki had vanished from the land as though they had never been.

The only living creature Wawasha found was a small brown papoose, forgotten in the headlong escape, who lay propped against a war-drum, smiling and sucking its thumb.

Wawasha took up this child, for like all his folk he regarded small ones as sacred and not to be harmed – unlike the early vikings who made what they called 'a clean sweep' of any town they captured. And Wawasha carried the baby boy back with him in the prow of his war-boat, fondling it with red hands, clucking and singing to it, to keep it from becoming afraid in the darkness.

And this child he gave to a young squaw whose husband had fallen in the first of the fighting that night. She called the boy by a name which meant 'Gift from the Gods', and was always happy with him, and he with her.

For a baby boy does not consider whether he is Algonkin or Beothuk; he sets store only by milk and mother-warmth. And gentle songs murmured in his ear when the fire glow dies at evening time.

When the morning light came again, so that the red men and the white men could see about them, they knew that they had paid well for that night's victory. Ten canoes had been sunk, and each one had held four braves. True, some of the braves were still there, but not in such wise as they might go hunting again, or singing again, or eating again.

The Algonkin were masters of axe and scalping-knife.

Gichita mourned, his robe over his head, while Wawasha, his forearms tied up with strips of cloth, tried to console him. The chief's legs had been cut across by a single blow of the war-axe and he could not rise; though the old squaw who attended him, putting herbs and mosses over the wounds, said that all would be well before the moon came to its full again.

Heome, once more despised because of his fear, sat alone, staring across the river waters, deep in his own despair, speaking to no one.

On *Long Snake* Harald and Grummoch took stock of their losses. Harald had a lump on the side of his head almost as big as a man's fist.

The giant said good-humouredly, 'Praise be to Odin, he gave thee a good hard Northern skull, oath-brother!'

Harald nodded, but did not speak. Instead, he pointed to Jamsgar Havvarson and Thorfinn Thorfinnson, who lay with their faces to the heavens, as though in a white sleep.

Grummoch said, 'Gudbrod Gudbrodsson will be lonely now. There were not such a pair this side of Valhalla while they lived. But look at the red men who lie beside them. They did not waste their time, those two.'

Then they saw the warrior Gudbrod, standing by the mast, the bodies of Algonkin and Abnaki heaped about him, and at first they thought he was sorrowing for the death of his friends, his head sunk on his breast.

But it was not sorrow which dragged his head down so, nor was he thinking of his dead friends, or of anything at all. Two Algonkin arrows held him upright to the mast, so that he did not fall with the rest.

Knud Ulfson sat by the shield-gunwales, binding his arm-wounds with rags and singing, his eyes wild still:

> 'When the young bucks go from the herd,
> Old stag fights on; he knows
> No rest from conflict. He
> Now runs across the hills,
> Sharp-horned and fiery-eyed,
> Seeking the killers, his chest
> Flecked with the froth of his anger.
> The stag, Knud Ulfson, says
> That now the young bucks have gone
> From the herd, he will run to the end
> Of the world, seeking the killers!'

Harald went over and patted him gently on the scarred shoulder.

'The killers have been paid, berserk,' he said. 'Their villages have been destroyed as though they had never been.'

But Knud Ulfson only looked up at him with empty eyes and half-open mouth, as though he did not understand the words his war-leader was speaking. Then he went back to his chanting, seeming to forget the very existence of Harald.

Grummoch said, 'There is little profit in talking to him yet. These berserks live in a closed world of conflict and brotherhood. It will be long before Knud Ulfson's ears will be open to the voices of men, for he is in the battle-trance yet, and I doubt whether he could see his hand before his face. That is the way of berserks.'

Harald said sadly, 'And look, we have lost four others. This is a dear price to pay for crushing the Algonkin and Abnaki on behalf of our red friends, the Beothuk.'

Grummoch said, pointing to a great man who hung half over the longship's prow, 'The enemy have paid dearly too, it seems.'

The two friends dragged the giant red man back into the ship and looked down at him.

From head to foot, he was garbed as only the greatest of chieftains could be. He wore an immense war bonnet of eagles' feathers, their tips dyed brown and garnished with red strands of hair, their bases fluffed out with the white down from the breast of the goose. About his throat was a necklace of a hundred bears' claws, each one set in silver and hanging from a thin hide string. His arms above the elbow were heavy with bands of copper, beaten and embossed with the sign of the great-winged thunderbird. His apron and breechclouts were smothered so with beads of red, and blue and yellow, that it would have been hard to get a lance-point between them. The shoes upon his feet bore the pattern of the rising sun, worked in thin strands of gold wire, against a sky of azure beads as small as an ant's head.

His face, caked with yellow clay, was still proud, even in the fearful sort of death the Northern axe had brought to him. He still held his feathered tomahawk in his right hand, as though prepared for anything on the long dark journey that lay before him.

Wawasha climbed over the side of the longship and gazed down at the dead red man.

'That is War Eagle,' he said. 'He was the greatest of all the Algonkin chieftains. Once he was my father's young friend, until they quarrelled over a squaw. Then they swore to kill each other. But my father, Gichita, still loved him, and would be hurt to the heart to know that War Eagle had died on your ship, from which his spirit may not rise to the Last Hunting Grounds. We must not tell him, for he has troubles enough.'

Then Wawasha bent and touched the Algonkin first on the right cheek, then on the left; then on the right breast, then on the left. And at last he knelt before the dead War Eagle and spoke softly to him, so that no one could hear, closing his proud eagle's eyes with gentle fingers.

And when he had done that, the vikings stripped the Algonkin of his fine clothes and then tied a piece of iron to his feet. They heaved him over the side of *Long Snake*, away from the canoe of Gichita, so that the old man should not be further troubled in his mind.

Later that day, they made a funeral pyre on the shore, beneath the heavy green boughs of the spruce trees, and so sent the dead vikings to Valhalla. The red men put their dead into the branches of the trees, seeing that each man's weapon lay across his lap, so that he should awake, ready for battle or hunting, when he came to the journey's end.

And that day, when the sun stood at its highest point in the blue sky, Gichita commanded that his son, Wawasha, should take Harald and Grummoch as his true blood-brothers.

A slit was made in the arm of each man by the medicine man, who bore bison horns on his headdress for the occasion, and their blood was intermingled as it flowed, so that some of Wawasha's seemed to enter the wounds of Harald and Grummoch. Then, holding hands, they were all three laid in a shallow trench, which the braves had dug in the soft ground above the shore; and then the turfs were lightly placed above them, so that they could not be seen.

This was the sign that as brothers they must live, and as brothers go into the earth together at the last call.

And when this was done, the Beothuk sang songs and danced, to the high wailing of the bone flute and the deep throbbing of the skin drum.

Only Heome showed no gladness, but sat alone among the squaws and the children, pale-faced and glowering.

Then came a long season of labour. Sometimes, to avoid the rushing, buffeting river, the red men took little streams that ran slower and curled round among overhanging tree-boughs. Once a creature like a great cat leapt down into a canoe, upsetting the braves into the water. They swam around the cat and struck it with tomahawks until it no longer showed its teeth at them or at anyone. The squaws and children in the other boats clapped their hands and laughed at this, and each cried out for the great skin to wear as a robe.

At other times they were faced by a wall of rock, down which the water thundered, white as ice; and then they had to pull ashore and carry their canoes on their shoulders up the slope and away from the waterfall. These were the hard times, for *Long Snake* was a mite too heavy to be hoisted upon shoulders and carried! It was then that the braves cut down tree-trunks and made rollers to go under the longship, and so, tugging on hide ropes, all the men and women helped the vikings to drag *Long Snake* up to the higher reaches of the river.

'We have known such portages in Russia,' said Harald. 'There was one such when we came back from Miklagard in the ships of Haakon Baconfat.'

'Hm,' said Grummoch, shielding his eyes and gazing at the immensely high wall of rock down which the river-water gushed. 'But it was not such a portage as this.

There cannot be such another portage as this in all the world!'

But they got to the top in the end, hands chafed raw, backs almost breaking, the blood singing in their heads. And at the top they made camp for that night, too tired to go any further up the great river.

Once, when they were resting so, at the edge of a pine-wood, the women tapping quietly on small skin drums while the older children danced about the fires, Heome leaped up and began to wave his arms about, his pale face bitter with anger.

'Why is it, my father,' he asked old Gichita, 'that these white strangers of the long wooden boat sit beside you and my brother Wawasha, at the fire, while I am given a place among the children? Have I not proved that I am a man, like the others?'

Gichita smiled sadly, his yellow face wrinkling in the firelight, and said gently, 'Heome, my son, I cannot over-throw the customs of our people by asking for what I desire or for what you desire. All men of the tribe know that I love both my sons with an equal love, as a father should. I care not if one is big and strong, the other small and weak. Among the bear folk the great father plays with the crippled cub just as he plays with the strong ones, who may grow to overthrow him one day.'

Heome said bitterly, in the firelight, 'Might not the crippled one overthrow him, too, by tricks the old bear did not think of?'

But Gichita, whose legs were troubling him, spoke on in some pain and said, 'It is true that you brought back a wolf which you killed in the forests near our home-place; but since then, we have met the Algonkin and the Abnaki, and men have said that then you did not act like a warrior, like the son of a chieftain. They say that while they were fighting, you lay among the deerhides in the boat, covering your face with your blanket, as though you were not there. That is why you sit where you do, about the fire; and there is nothing I can do, Heome, until your chance comes again to prove yourself. Then, my son, you too shall sit beside me with the others; and you, too, shall take the oath of blood-brotherhood with the great white warriors here, and shall lie with them under the turf.'

Heome gave a high shrill cry and said, 'I would rather die, Gichita, than stoop to claim brotherhood with these strangers, who are white wolves and nothing more ... white wolves who come with us for what they can get, not from any love of our people !'

Harald and Grummoch sat silent at the fire, staring at Heome, who would not meet their eyes; but others of the vikings were not so calm. Some said that they had lost good men, fighting a battle which was none of their business. Others said that if they had had their way, *Long Snake* would now be halfway home to the Northland.

But in the end Wawasha quietened them all by getting up and performing the Eagle Dance, spreading his arms wide, making a wide and leaping circle, as though the bird he represented was hovering above the fire, and all the time calling out, 'Ku-e-e-e !'

The women about the far fires took up this call – 'Ku-e-e-e ! Ku-e-e-e !' until the woodlands echoed and re-echoed with the sound.

Then, as the drum-sticks of green ash and hickory

pattered out the delicate cross-beats of this dance, Wawasha stopped, poised high on his toes, raised his arms, quivering, as though they were truly wings, and let his finger-tips touch lightly above his head.

In the dead silence of the climax of this dance, Heome rose and spat into the fire, contemptuously.

But no one regarded him, their eyes were fixed on the young warrior who would one day become their chieftain.

Suddenly, when Wawasha was at his full height, the drums beat out a loud and concerted *twang!* as though a gigantic bow-string had been released.

Then, in the silence which followed, Wawasha gave a high scream, 'Ku-e-e-e-ok!', fluttered wildly in a circle, always sinking lower and lower towards the ground as he moved round the fires, until at length he fell to the turf, one wing still beating in spasms.

At last this arm sank, too, and the drumming became softer and softer, until it was little more than a whisper, dying away with the dying of the bird.

The women's eyes glistened with tears. The children crept closer to them, snuggling their heads within the buckskin blouses of their mothers. Only the braves still stared at the motionless figure of Wawasha, their copper faces blank and impassive, expressing their admiration by silence.

Gichita bowed his old head and spoke a prayer to the Eagle God:

'Thunderbirdman! O Thunderbirdman!
We worship you!
We of the Beothuk look to you for aid!
See that we journey well, O Thunderbirdman!

See that we reach our cooking-place safely !
That is all we ask, O Thunderbirdman !'

Then Wawasha rose and went to his father, smiling.

'Did the dance go well, Father Gichita?' he asked.

The old man nodded. 'It went well, my son,' he said. 'I feel in my heart now that we shall live to see the Great Lakes and the sacred stone quarries !'

But Harald whispered to Grummoch, 'I should feel happier if that mad wolf, Heome, were tied up safely with a chain about his neck, so that we could always know what he was up to. Last night I dreamed that he was standing on the waters of the river, speaking with the Shield-maiden who once came to visit me out of the mist, after I left Havlock Ingolfson to drown on the rocky skerry in the mist. In my dream, it seemed that Heome and the Shield-maiden came to some agreement for they took each other by the hand, and smiled a great deal. The strange thing is that Heome's crippled hand seemed to come alive again, to have movement in its fingers, as he reached forth to clasp the white hand of the Shield-maiden.'

Grummoch said, 'Dreams are not always to be trusted. I once dreamed I had a new sword and axe, studded with rubies from Miklagard. I tell you, those weapons were as clear to my mind as anything I have ever seen. Even in my dream, I felt that if I touched them on the edge, they would cut my hand. Yet, what happened? When I awoke and felt under my bench, where they were supposed to lie – they were not there ! Nor have I ever been given them ! Nay, Harald, dreams are not to be trusted. Think no more of Heome the Wolf. If he becomes too dangerous, I will suggest to Knud Ulfson, the berserk, that he takes friend Heome into the woods and shows him the path to Valhalla – with a little knife. No doubt, it would be a task which Knud would enjoy, for he thinks of little else but that sort of thing. We cannot get him to row or to pull on ropes! He should do *something* for his living!'

Harald turned away without answering, for he felt that it would ill become a fighter like Knud Ulfson to kill the crippled son of Gichita, however venomous he became.

However, Knud Ulfson was put to another task the next day, which was greatly to his taste, and which came as a complete surprise to him and to everyone else.

He was out strolling through the woods alongside the river, when all others were rowing upstream, when a red man dropped out of a tree and struck at him with a war-club.

Now Knud Ulfson was not a man to refuse battle to anyone, so he let the club sweep over his bent back, and then he kicked the red man's feet from under him.

What he did with his axe then, neither he nor anyone else recalled. The red man who lay at his feet never knew, anyway.

And when Knud had sung a little song about his own skill as a warrior, he stripped the brave of his headdress and buckskin waistcoat embroidered with red and yellow beads, and then put them on, for he liked finery, having so long lived a pretty poor life on this long voyage.

When at length he caught up with *Long Snake*, which was fighting against the swirling waters of the rapids, many of the vikings cried out that here was a white-skinned red man – until they saw his long yellow plaits and recognized him.

Wawasha smiled grimly and said, 'You wear the clothes of a chieftain's son. That is Oneida bead-work. It is very pretty.'

Knud Ulfson preened himself and shook out his great feathered headdress, then answered, 'The man who wore them did not deserve them. Who wears such finery should fight with more skill.'

Nor would he say more than that. But Wawasha said to Harald, 'If your man has killed a son of the Oneida, then we had best move swiftly, for they are a revengeful people, and will not sit by their fires singing peace-songs when once they know what has happened.'

After that *Long Snake* and all the canoes went forward, by day and by night, until they thought they were out of Oneida territory.

Once, however, they were forced to rest the night, in a little basin, overhung by spruce trees, for Gichita's right leg had swollen badly and was red and inflamed. An old woman of the Beothuk, who had great art in dressing wounds, said that the swelling would not go down unless Gichita lay the whole of one night with the skin of the green snake wrapped about his leg.

Though the old man shook his head and said that he did not wish to hold up the journey, especially in such a perilous place, the young braves refused for once to obey him and laid down their paddles. Some of them went off into the woods and after much searching came back with three little green snakes, which were skinned that night and the skins bound round the wound while they still held their moisture.

That night a party of red men wearing heavy bear-skin robes came down to the basin and sat beside the canoes, their war-axes ready on their knees, their faces flat and motionless, their dark eyes like slits in a deerhide.

And when Wawasha awoke and looked around for the guards he had placed about the camp, the leader of the men in bear-skins said, 'Do not blame your guards, friend. We crept upon them and tied them to trees. They are not harmed, nor will you be harmed, if you are men of sense.'

'Who are you?' asked Wawasha. 'I do not know your language, yet I understand a word here and there.'

The other said, 'We are Swamp Cree, my friend, and have lost our tracks through this woodland. To us, every tree seems like its fellow. We are not used to wandering through forests.'

Wawasha nodded. 'What do you want, men of the Swamp Cree?'

The man said, 'We want to go to the pipestone quarries beside the Big Lake, but we do not know the way. Our way lies further north and we have lost it. Let us travel with you, and all will be well.'

Wawasha said, 'It is not wise to speak threateningly to us Beothuk, my friend. We have gods travelling with us in their great ship of wood. If they woke and heard you speak too proudly, they might decide to lessen you in height by the length of a head, or in number by a few dozen.'

The Swamp Cree gazed back at Wawasha, their lips drawn down in a smile of disbelief. Wawasha whistled three times then, and Grummoch, who was a light sleeper, leaped on shore and strode to where the Swamp Cree squatted, their axes across their knees.

He stood the height of a man and half a man, and was as broad as three men. He wore an iron helmet, at the sides of which sprouted out the black horns of a bull. About his body he wore a rusty iron hauberk. His axe was so heavy that few men could swing it.

And when Grummoch strode among them, the Swamp Cree drew back, gasping, though too brave to show fear.

Grummoch said, 'What! Have the bears come to break their fast with us, or on us, Wawasha, my brother?'

Wawasha said, for all to hear, 'It is for them to decide. If they choose the first, there is deer-meat for them; if they choose the second, there is death.'

Grummoch nodded lazily, and began to swing his great axe, *Death Kiss*, in the pale dawn air, as though this were a matter of little importance. The axe made a whistling sound as it swung and the Swamp Cree watched with admiration.

At last their chief said, smiling wryly, 'This fellow is not one I would care to offend, unless I had my ten brothers with me!'

Grummoch stopped swinging his axe and said, 'I beg you, go and fetch your ten brothers. I will sit here on this stone until they come. I do not run away from a challenge.'

But the Swamp Cree shook his grizzled head and answered, 'In the north, we are a great folk, and are respected by all, even by the Big Innuit. We wish to remain so, which might not be if we had the ill luck to let your axe fall on our necks too often. Look you, white god, let us travel with you, and we will fight with you if the need arises. Is that a bargain?'

Wawasha nodded, so Grummoch agreed, too, for in truth he had not wanted to fight so early in the morning, before he had eaten his breakfast.

Then Harald and the other vikings came and sat down with the Beothuk and the Swamp Cree, about a great fire, while Gichita watched, smiling, for his swelling had now gone down and his leg had lost its redness, just as the old woman had promised.

Then the chief of the Swamp Cree took from his inner tunic a long hollow rod of black wood, to the end of which he fitted a carved red-stone bowl. And into this bowl he sifted grains and shreds of a dried herb. And when this was done, he set fire to the herb and sucked at the black rod of wood. Smoke came out of his mouth.

Knud Ulfson said, 'By Thor, but this is strange magic! Never have I seen smoke in a man's mouth before. Does it not burn his inner cheeks, Wawasha?'

Wawasha said, 'No man has been burned by it yet. Though it is not a custom my folk are given to. Yet they blow the smoke out of their mouths when they are required to do so by other tribes who use the pipe; for it is a sign of peace.'

Then the chief of the Swamp Cree passed the smoking pipe to Grummoch and signed that he should do as he had already done.

The giant gave a great suck at the hollow rod, and then began to cough as though he would die, for he had forgotten to blow out the smoke and had swallowed it, as he would have done a draught of mead.

Now all the red men laughed, and one of the Swamp

Cree even dared to go forward and slap Grummoch on the back. Though he made a wry face as he did so, for Grummoch's back in its iron coat was as hard as a barn door made of solid oak.

So, among laughter, the pipe was passed back and forth among the leaders. Knud Ulfson took it and blew out the longest stream of all.

'This is child's play,' he shouted. 'Why, I dare eat the pipe, fire and all!'

But Harald stopped him with a black look, for the berserk was liable to do anything he said he would, regardless of the wisdom or foolishness of his promise.

At last the pipe went back into the robe of the leader of the Swamp Cree, whose name was Lanook; and so the two parties of red men travelled as one from that time, the Beothuk and the Swamp Cree.

Until at last, one bright morning, they sailed round a bend in the river and then stopped, stricken with awe by the sight that met their eyes.

Before them lay the waters of the Big Lake, so broad that it might have been a sea, for it was impossible to see to its furthermost shore. Waves rippled across the deep green waters, and great trees floated on it, like longships, here and there.

Harald said, 'I have travelled through Finmark, and know the lakes there; but to this one, they are nothing but puddles left by the rain!'

Grummoch asked Wawasha, 'Are these waters indeed those of a lake, or those of the sea? I can scarcely believe that a lake could be so immense.'

Wawasha said, 'This is a lake, my friend. The Lake of the Gods. But it is not the end of our journey, for we must pass through this lake, and then into another, and yet another until we come to the greatest of them all — and then we shall reach the gathering-place of the tribes. That is the end of our journey.'

Chapter **20** *The Gathering-Place of the Tribes*

Now in the full summer when the eagle flung himself across the sky for the sheer fury of living, and the sun seemed to burn brighter with every day, the Beothuk and the Swamp Cree set up their buffalo-hide tepees, each one the height of three men standing on each other's shoulders. These skin houses were painted with bright colours, and had their smoke-holes facing towards the east, for the wind which most commonly blew across the Plains came from the west.

Along the shores of the greatest lake, and stretching inland beyond all woods and across the wide prairies, tribes had set up their tepees, until it seemed that all the red men in the world had gathered there to hunt the horned buffalo and to dig the red stone from the sacred quarries.

Harald and the vikings stood on the deck of *Long Snake* and looked outwards, at the multitude of tepees and the great clouds of dust and smoke that rose above the plain. They shut their eyes and listened to the myriad sounds of a great community – the shouting of men, the lowing of cattle, the squealing of children, the yelping of dogs, the singing of women, the sound of axe on wood, the drumming, the fluting, the pounding of feet. . . .

Grummoch said, 'Never did I expect to see and hear such a vast multitude. In Caledonia, when the geese gather to fly away for the winter, we children used to think that nowhere in all the world could so many creatures mass together and move away. But if all the geese that have lived since the beginning of time could gather and fly, there would not be such a number as these red folk.'

Harald said, dreamily, 'If one could carry this great host back to the Northland, and set spears and real iron axes in their hands, what might one not do! The warlord who led such a host might conquer England, Frankland, Miklagard, Spain, oh, everywhere! Such a lord would be the greatest the world had ever known, brothers!'

Knud Ulfson said, 'My father once led a war-party of Irishmen and Danes and Icelanders on a foray against the Franks. But the result was that they cut each other's throats, and my father was left in Frankland with a leaking boat and only the rusty sword he carried, to gain his fortune. It took him three years to walk back home. Nay, I for one would not wish to be the war-lord of such a varied folk as these red men, who seem more apt at cutting throats than most folk I have met.'

When the vikings went to the great tepee of Gichita, they found that he was holding a council with the chieftains of the other red folk. He lay back in his litter, for his legs still troubled him so much that he could not stand on them for long at a time, surrounded by the stoutest of his warriors.

The other chieftains passed a stone peace-pipe round the fire, grunting and nodding, their black eyes expressionless, even when the white vikings arrived and ranged themselves behind Gichita.

Harald gazed round the great circle with astonishment. He had not thought that men could be so different, one from the other. In that crowd were small men, as yellow and flat-faced as the Innuit, and wearing bearskins with the hide outermost; tall brown men, who hardly wore anything at all, save a bead loin-cloth and copper arm-bands and a small sheaf of arrows slung before their chests; sturdy men with beaded waistcoats and moccasins, high headdresses of eagles' feathers, and carrying feathered lances and fur-trimmed bucklers; men of all sorts, of all tribes. Gichita spoke to them in a simple language, helped out by signs of the hands and the head. They anwered by nodding, or by making gestures with hand and arm.

Wawasha whispered to Harald, 'We are the last folk to arrive, and so must give an explanation of our journey. That is why Gichita, my father, is addressing them. It is the custom. The language he speaks is the "first language", as we call it; it is the tongue the first red men brought with them when they came, a thousand men's lives ago, over the northern ice with their packs on their backs, to settle here in woodland and forest, in desert and by seashore. All red men know this "first language" and use it when they speak together, at this time of the year. It is the language of peace and of brotherhood. Later, when we leave the red stone quarries and go back to our own cooking-places, we shall speak our own tongue, Beothuk and Algonkin and Oneida, not the "first language".'

Harald said, 'Does that mean that when you all leave this place, you will kill each other again?'

Wawasha nodded. 'That is the old custom,' he said.

'We all move out from the quarries on the same day, when the first breath of winter begins to blow, and make our way homewards. It is the old law that for three days, no man may fight with another. After that, when the red folk are well away from the sacred place, they may please themselves.'

Grummoch said, 'This is not an unusual notion. The folk south of Miklagard who make their yearly journey to Jerusalem, where their sacred place is, do likewise; and so do the Franks and the Avars and the Saxons, when they go to Rome, I have heard. It is a convenient arrangement, and results in less shedding of blood than might be the case if there were no such law.'

Wawasha smiled grimly and said, 'Even so, there are those who drink the maize beer about their fires at night and forget the old law. Then they dance until they have forgotten what they are about, and their next idea is to raid the tepees of any tribe they hate.'

Knud Ulfson said, 'That I can understand, coming from a family of berserks myself. The joy of life lies not in sitting about a hearth-stone, listening to the tales of old women, but in swapping blows with other men, and laying one's enemies at one's feet. That is the true joy of life.'

Harald Sigurdson looked at him sternly and said, 'I have a wife and two sons, who live beside the fjord and wait for me to return one day. It is my intention to go back to them, and so I will have no more of this berserk talk, Knud Ulfson. What your family did is one thing; what I command you to do is another. So have the goodness to keep away from maize beer and dancing while we are with these red men. And keep your axe where it belongs, on the thong at your side. If ever I see you putting on that daft berserk look, I shall save the red men the trouble and will silence you myself. Remember that!'

Knud Ulfson did not like those words; but he knew that Harald Sigurdson never spoke unless he meant what he said. Indeed, along the fjord there was a fire-saying which went:

> 'Thunder threatens but may not strike;
> Rain threatens but may blow over;
> Wolf snarls but may not bite;
> When Harald snarls, your life is over.'

So Knud bowed his head and turned away, anxious not to see the snarl appear on the face of Sigurdson.

That night there was much singing and dancing, to the many talking-drums and the wood and bone flutes. In the firelight a long line of red men from the far south stood, mother-naked, whirling great bull-roarers about their heads, until the purple dusk was alive with the whirring, thrumming, murmuring of these instruments. Beyond the firelight a group of red men from the western shores danced in a ring, their backs garnished with a circle of painted feathers to represent the sun. The sound of their feet beat out a rhythm which seemed to throb through the earth itself and then crept upwards into everyone's bones.

Harald, wandering among the many groups of red men, noticed Knud Ulfson drinking deep from a great earthen jar, held to his lips by a smiling red man whose face was decorated with bars of white ochre. Knud was shuddering as he drank, and Harald knew this to be a bad sign.

Gently he took the jar from the berserk and handed it back politely to the red man, who stared up at him half dazed. Then Harald took Knud by the neck and led him to a high totem-pole which was set firmly in the earth, and there he tied Knud Ulfson by the hands, to the pole, with thongs of wet deerhide, until the morning.

When he came to set Knud free, he saw that the berserk had gnawed the painted wood like a savage dog. But when Knud looked into Harald's eyes, he bent his head as though ashamed of himself.

Harald said, 'If I see you drinking maize beer again, I shall bring peace to you suddenly. Is that understood, berserk?'

Knud Ulfson said, 'It is understood, shipmaster. I will abide by it – though I feel that such laws are unmanly and unreasonable.'

Harald gave him a smack that almost laid him flat, and said, 'While I am the master of *Long Snake*, I will not be told what I am to do by any seal-brained berserk from the fjords. Now get you gone and sleep off your madness.'

Later in the day, Grummoch came to Harald and said, 'It ill becomes a viking to set great store by trifles – but today I have seen a strange sight.'

Grummoch waited for Harald to ask him what the strange sight might be, for that was the manner of Northmen when they had interesting news to disclose. But Harald merely sat and smiled at him, until the giant could stand this scrutiny no longer and said, 'There is danger brewing, Harald Sigurdson. Mark my words, and I do not speak lightly.'

Then Harald said, 'What is the danger, Little One? I

am always anxious to hear of danger, for it gives spice to my meat.'

Grummoch said with a frown, 'This danger may not be to your taste, oath-brother. Heome has sworn a brotherhood with that fool, Knud Ulfson. He has caused Knud to forget his oath to you, in his battle-madness. Heome has said to him that Knud shall be his hands and his arms, and in return for what he is to do, Knud shall be named the greatest berserk of all the red men. I heard all this in the forest when I bent behind a bush to fasten up my shoestrings.'

Harald was silent for a while, and then at length he asked, 'And what does Heome wish daft Knud to do, then, oath-brother?'

Grummoch answered, 'He has asked him to destroy his own brother, Wawasha, and his old father, Gichita. That is all.'

Harald said, 'And that is quite enough. We must keep a steady eye on those two fools now, for such a pact could mean our own end, too.'

'That is what I thought,' said Grummoch, slyly, 'but I did not like to suggest it, being but a simple giant, as you remind me so often, and you such a man of cleverness and great affairs.'

Harald gave him a grim look, but said nothing.

Chapter 21 *Strange Partners*

Then followed a time of fishing, when the many red folk dragged nets through the shallow pools, or rode in their birch-bark boats over the lake-waters with their sharp fish-spears poised. Sometimes this happened at nightfall,

when the fish little suspected their attackers; and then the rolling lake seemed like a place of magic, with the bobbing torches and the men in their white-clayed buffalo-robes, standing, ghostwise, in their boats, their many-pronged hardwood lances held at the ready.

And after that, the buffalo hunting.

In and out of the great shag-haired herds ran the lithest of the hunters, the wind in their impassive faces, their lances thrusting hither and thither among the heaving stupid beasts.

Often, after such a raid, the plains were dotted thickly with immense brown bodies, just as though it were a battlefield of giants, and the giants had come off the worst of the encounter.

Though sometimes the red men suffered, too, as when a woodland tribe, little accustomed to this hunting sport, allowed itself to be caught in a narrow sandstone gully, when the furious frightened herd crashed through in terror, pursued by other men and dogs. That day the Seminole, a simple swamp folk, who seldom made the long journey to the sacred quarries because of the distance, mourned their many crushed dead. Hardly one of them could be recognized, so harshly had the hooves treated them.

Grummoch had great taste for this sport, being swift of foot and strong of the lance-thrust. During that time, he alone killed two score of the lumbering creatures, moving amongst them as he would do in a battle with men, striking to left and to right, then jumping clear of the wildly tossing heads, the fiercely threshing hooves, the agonized twisting of the great bodies which could crush a man.

Among the many red men, Grummoch became known as 'Bull Killer', and at least four of the tribes sent deputations to him, asking him to hunt with them and to live in their lodges.

Always Grummoch shook his own great shaggy head with courtesy and said, 'I have lord and lodge already. It ill becomes a man to change his chieftain.'

Harald was likewise held in great respect by the red

folk, for in a shallow valley, darkened by overhanging thorn-bushes, he had stumbled on a nest of poisonous snakes, and had trodden each one of them into the ground fearlessly, before they had had time to sink their fangs in his legs or feet.

For this he was named 'Snake Destroyer', and given snakeskin arm-bands by the troop of Ojibiweg who had watched this strange encounter.

And always, when the vikings gained fame in this manner, Wawasha and his father Gichita called the Beothuk together about the fires and ordered dancing and drumming. The drums of all shapes and colours were seldom silent in that encampment.

And always, when such feastings took place, Heome Nohands went away to the lakeside and wept, beyond the power of man to soothe, praying bitterly to his private gods that the strangers who had belittled him, by being so strong themselves, should suffer. Yet, now, he had learned to smile when he spoke to his brother, and Harald, and Grummoch, so covering the bitter heart-thoughts that he held against them. And in his dreams, he saw the three of them drowning in the lake, or crushed under a fall of rocks in the quarries, or trampled down by the wild buffalo on the plains. Always he saw them dead and out of the way, so that he alone could gain the love of his tribe, and of his father, Gichita, without having to kill him. . . .

Then, at last, when the moon was at her full, the great medicine man of all the red folk sent round the chopping-axe of staghorn among the multitude of tepees, as a sign that the sacred red pipestone was ready to be quarried, and each tribe made its own plans to go to the quarries, unarmed, save with staghorn picks, and to dig what they needed in the coming year, for the making of pipes and beads and images, arm-bands for the young squaws and ear-rings for the young braves. This was an order which had never been disobeyed since the red folk came across the far northern ice with their bundles on their backs, thousands of lifetimes ago.

Before dawn the following day, the men of Gichita's tribe, together with the Swamp Cree and the vikings, rose silently and broke their fast, but carried neither food nor water with them; for it was the law that the diggers of the sacred stone should neither eat nor drink until they had returned to their lodges in the evening.

Grummoch tore at a great hunk of buffalo-meat, saying, 'Well, if I may not eat until sunset, I will make good use of my teeth now!'

Wawasha smiled and slapped him on the back. 'We have a saying,' he said, 'that big eaters make small diggers. See that your pick sinks deeper than any other man's today, for you have eaten more than anyone else of the tribe!'

Grummoch pretended to look offended and answered, 'If that is how you feel, then I will carry a buffalo with me, on my shoulder, to nibble on the way! A fellow must keep his strength up, my friend!'

The sacred stone quarries lay two leagues away from the lake, and Wawasha was anxious that his folk should get there to find a good digging-spot before all the other red folk took the best places. He hurried them along as much as he dared, seeing that every man had his staghorn pick and a buckskin bag into which he would put his diggings.

Between the tepees he met Harald and said, 'I have been searching for my brother, Heome, but cannot find him. He is not in his tent. That is strange, for every year he has gone with the others, and, though he cannot dig, he has spoken the prayers of our people as his part of the ceremony.'

Harald said, just as solemnly, 'My man, Knud Ulfson, is nowhere to be found, either. That, too, is strange; for always he has been at my back, since we left the North-lands. Do you think they may have gone together to the quarries, unwilling to wait for us?'

Wawasha thought for a while, his chin in his copper-coloured hand, and then he said, 'They may indeed have gone together, and mean to wait for us. But, if so, they have gone alone, for none of our tribe is missing, and two lone dogs like that will drag down few deer, it seems to me.'

Then the two men said no more, but began the long run towards the stone quarries before the other tribes should wake.

For some time they saw no one since they had set off at such an early hour, and at last their way ran beside a swampy stream, in a little gully, where the grass grew rank and stinking from the brackish water and the dead creatures which had gone there with arrows in their sides, or sinking from some disease, such as that fever which comes of eating the Juraba plant.

It was not a pleasant place to find oneself in, as all the vikings agreed. Here trolls might lurk, they said to each other. As for the Beothuk, they blew down their nostrils frequently, so that the spirit of the place might not enter their hearts and poison them.

But the Swamp Cree were accustomed to such places, and they trotted on, smiling, as though there was nothing in the tangled roots and slithering creatures to trouble a man.

In a thorn bush which stood above them, on the skyline, a bird suddenly screeched. The running party stopped and looked up. It was a swamp hawk, its feathers tattered and torn, as though it had suffered many conflicts with the other birds of the plains and marshes.

Wawasha said, 'Those birds are usually brave. It is not often that one hears them cry out when a man approaches. Perhaps it is an omen, my friends.'

Harald, who ran beside him, said, 'It ill becomes a man to stop in his running because an old bird suddenly feels the sadness of its life.'

But Wawasha said, 'We of the red folk learn to listen to the words of the creatures. And this creature tells me that it is disturbed in its heart. I would say that it has been made afraid this morning, by others than us.'

They ran on then, but Harald thought of Knud Ulfson, who was such a man as might trouble more than a mere bird, when he was in a mood to do so.

A little later, one of the Swamp Cree ran up to Wawasha and showed him a copper arm-band, thick with swamp mud.

'This I found beside the waters, chieftain's son,' he said.

Wawasha answered, 'This belongs to my brother, Heome. We must go carefully, my friends, from this point onwards. The gods have spoken to us twice; once through a bird, once through an arm-band. It would be foolish to shut our ears and our eyes to such signs.'

Grummoch said, 'They are two and we are many. For my part, I would as well run singing at the top of my voice. Who can harm us, when all folk go to the quarries without knife, or sword, or axe?'

Wawasha said nothing, but from then on he ran cautiously, sometimes watching the ground for spoors; sometimes swinging his fine head from side to side, like a questing beast.

But nothing happened, and at last they came out of the long valley where the swamp water stank and the flies buzzed, to see ahead of them on the top of the slope, a high and circular mound of clay. It stood against the blue sky like a smoothly-polished helmet, and looked to be big enough for forty men to stand upon in comfort, without jostling each other.

'That is an ancient burial mound,' said Wawasha. 'It was there before the first of the red folk came, and our tales say that it will still be there when the last of us have gone away from the land.'

Harald said, 'In England, in the south, there is a circle of great stones, about which men say the same thing. It was there before the Romans came, and it will be there when Odin decides to crumble the world in his two great hands. There are some such monuments which are meant to teach man that he is but a little thing, with a life hardly longer than that of a spring fly.'

They said no more, but set their course towards the ancient burial heap, beyond which lay steps, cut in the rock, leading down to the sacred quarries.

When at last they arrived at the tumulus, most of the men were glad, for they had somehow expected to be delayed, with one thing or another.

And so they scrambled up the smooth slopes with relief, at last standing on the summit and gazing below them, for a distance greater than ten men could shoot with one arrow after another.

Harald almost gasped with sheer amazement at the size and beauty of the great quarry, for he had never seen its like, in all his journeyings across the world.

It lay, like an immense hole scooped from the earth by the greatest hand of the greatest god the earth had ever known. A city ten times as great as Miklagard might have been placed within it, and then have left space for Rome. It was deep, deep, deep – deeper than the waters of the Jimjefjord, which, as all Northmen know, has no bottom. And its sides were sheer, save for the yellow bushes which sprouted here and there like the tufts of beard on an old man's cheeks. Its stone was of many colours – red, yellow, black, blue. The vikings cried aloud and said that this must be the end of the world, for they had seen no place like it, nor had heard of any in all the sagas they knew.

Wawasha pointed to a place a hundred paces away.

'That is the only way down,' he said. 'There are steps there which were cut when my grandfather's great-grandfathers first came here, when the sun was young and so small that a man could hold it in his hand without being burned. That is the place we must go to. All the tribes use those steps. We call them "The Steps to Life and Death". Let us go down! None of the other tribes will be here for another hour yet!'

As he spoke, they all stood on the mound-top, against the blue morning sky, their buckskin bags and staghorn picks in their hands.

And as he spoke, Wawasha suddenly let fall his pick and bag and gave a strange sobbing cry, then half-turned and flung his arms out wide. Harald and Grummoch, who stood on either side of him, caught him in their arms and gazed at him in amazement. Then they saw that a little arrow, hardly longer than a man's hand, stuck deep in his head, just above the right eye. There was little comfort to be had from asking Wawasha any questions, for his jaw had dropped and his eyes had rolled back sightless. In that one moment he had died, and now lay as heavily as three men, his great arms hanging useless before him.

Harald turned to Grummoch and was about to speak some words of astonishment, when from the lip of the sacred quarry, men began to run towards them, men of the Algonkin, the Abnaki, the Oneida, all swinging spears or tomahawks, all painted with the white and yellow war-ochre. And at the head of this pack of warrior-hounds ran Heome and Knud Ulfson, shouting like berserks, calling down death on all the men who stood on that ancient mound, their hands grasping short picks of staghorn, their hearts full of foreboding.

Grummoch gasped, 'By Thor, we are ambushed! Form a ring about the head of the mound, and strike with what you have! This is the warning that the swamp hawk spoke to us, though we had not ears to hear it then!'

And so the red men and the white men gathered, close to each other, like buffalo waiting for the slaughter.

Now, with the yapping of foxes and the deep and terrible grunting of bears, the attacking red men came in, striking low with their tomahawks, thrusting up viciously with feathered lances.

Grummoch, who stood well to the forefront, his tawny hair flying in the high breeze on the tumulus, shouted out, 'Come forth without delay, all who wish to try their skulls against this little horn-pick! The play has just begun, catch me while the mood is on me to strike once only and cleanly; later, my blows may grow careless, then meeting will give little pleasure to either side!'

The vikings around him laughed and cried out, 'Where are the famous Algonkin now?'

A tall young brave of the Algonkin, wearing a high fur hat stuck round with hawk's feathers dyed yellow, called back, 'We are here, pale murder-wolves! Have no fear, we shall come at you as soon as there is room to move!'

The Swamp Cree set their brown faces grimly and struck slowly and surely, each man grunting out the number of those who fell before his staghorn pick. But they were hampered by their heavy furs, and the attacking Abnaki on that side of the mound gave them small chance to strip off their clothes and to move freely.

The Swamp Cree suffered bitter losses that bright

morning, used as they were to a different manner of combat. But the Beothuk sucked in their breath and dilated their nostrils with contempt for their enemies; and soon the Algonkin learned that the little pick of staghorn, used with craft, can equal the copper-headed tomahawk, while its point lasts and its stave remains whole.

Harald, facing the Algonkin with the high fur cap, fending blows, striking blows by turn, saw from the edge of his eye a young viking named Olaf Miklofsson take a stroke from an Abnaki axe on the shaft of his pick, then kick upwards into his opponent's chest with such force that the man fell backwards, to be lanced through by the oncoming Indians. Almost immediately afterwards, Olaf Miklofsson was struck on the neckbone by an Abnaki who had pushed his way among the Swamp Cree and was standing in the midst of the men on the burial mound.

Harald shouted out, 'Stand back to back, you red men, then they cannot come amongst us so !'

The great Algonkin who faced him bellowed out that the white men were cowards, and drove at Harald's shoulder with his long-bladed axe.

Harald said, 'A little more to the left would have been better, friend !' And swaying from the blow he slashed sideways so that the sharp-pointed pick entered the Algonkin's side, between the lower ribs.

The warrior fell sideways, dragging with him Harald's pick, its shaft now slippery with sweat and other things. Harald bent swiftly and snatched the long-bladed war-axe from the dying brave's hand.

'Exchange is no robbery, friend !' he said grimly, and then turned to ward off the blows of another red man.

Grummoch saw this happen and said, 'When I go back home to the fjord, I shall tell all I meet that Harald Sigurdson is so crafty a bargainer that he even sets up his market stall on the battlefield!'

This was meant to be a taunt, but Harald took it otherwise, as is the right way among warriors at such a time; and he answered, 'It would well become Grummoch of the rusty hair to call a higher price for his blows. He is letting them go too cheaply, and half his enemies are escaping with little more than a broken arm or a cracked head!'

Grummoch was indeed so sorely pressed that often he had to let his opponents stagger away without the end-knock which he was used to giving on all occasions, wherever possible.

Indeed, at the moment when Harald spoke, three red men were about the giant, stabbing with lances, almost cutting each other in their haste to be at the giant.

Harald stepped forward and sliced down at two of them before they knew where he was. The third, seeing that now he stood against two of the white warriors, swung about and rolled down the hillock into safety for the time being.

The vikings laughed and slapped each other on the shoulders. Then Grummoch stopped and chose for himself the best and the longest of the lances dropped by the fallen red men.

'Now we are well-armed for such as will come against us,' he said. 'And thank you, oath-brother, for that bit of advice about bargaining. I have never before needed to trade my weapons in battle, and the wisdom of your words came at a good time.'

Harald said, 'I am always pleased to advise a friend on such occasions.'

Then, in the little lull that followed, Grummoch pointed over the black heads of the swaying red men and said, 'Look at the edge of the crowd. Heome and Knud Ulfson are there; I wondered when we should see them again !'

Heome was beating on a shallow drum with his nerveless hands, since he could not hold a drumstick. The rhythms he was evoking from the stretched deerhide came over the littered ground like the mutterings of death.

Knud Ulfson had torn off every stitch of clothing, and was nodding his head back and forth in time to the drum, like a war-stallion that can hardly be restrained from plunging, blind, into the thick of the fighting. His plaits, which were usually yellow, were now stained red, and flopped stiffly behind him. His right hand clutched a long iron axe that he had brought from the ship. On his left arm was a round buckler, such as the red men carry; a thing of wood, covered with buffalo-hide and edged about with the down of the winter goose.

Grummoch said bitterly, 'It ill becomes a viking to strike against his kith and kin. Yonder youth is drunk with more than maize beer this time. Now he is thirsty for honour among the Algonkin ! I think he looks to be their war chief when this affair is over !'

Harald said grimly, 'At the end of this morning, Knud Ulfson will lie stark upon this mound. That I promise you, and I do not speak hastily in these matters.'

Grummoch, whose arms were red to the elbows, and whose broad face was streaked with blood and sweat, yelled out then, 'Knud Ulfson, I bear an invitation to a party! Come up here like a man and let us dance together, my friend!'

Knud gazed about him, blank-eyed as a blind man, and called back into the blue air, 'I am Loki now, the red one. Crippled Hoder beats the drum for me, because proud Balder is dead! I come to no man's bidding!'

Harald said, 'The poor fool is quite mad, as mad as the red man who has brought this battle about!'

Then, raising his voice, he shouted to Knud, 'Ulfson, little man, Harald Sigurdson commands you! Come up the hill and show him what you still know of axe-usage, for, remember, it was Harald who taught you all you know, in the pasture-field behind the village middens!'

Knud Ulfson gave a little shuffle of the feet, as though he might be about to fall down, then he waved his bloody head from side to side, mincingly, like a girl who is petulant, and cares not who sees it.

And at last he called out in a high, unnatural voice, 'Harald Sigurdson is a man! I will not harm Harald Sigurdson, who taught me all I know of the axe-play! Let Harald Sigurdson come down the hill and stand by my side as my brother and he and I will fight for Heome together! Two true berserks among a pack of mangy wolves!'

Harald Sigurdson replied, 'I take only men as my brothers, Ulfson Maidenhair! I fight only for men, and Heome Tenderhand is not my man! Come forth, Ulfson, and learn what it is to face a man!'

Then the red men on the hillock began to laugh in mockery, though they stood knee high among the bodies of their dearest brothers, and their own strength was failing as the sun climbed higher in the blue sky.

Knud Ulfson heard this laughter and began to grit his teeth so savagely that pieces of them broke off. He began to bite his lips with such abandon that his own blood ran down his long chin, giving him a red beard. He began to swing his long-shafted iron axe so perilously that all the red men stood away from him, knowing in their own savage way that he was now beyond speech and reasoning.

Then Knud began to cry out, to the beat of Heome's little drum, which stuttered with the berserk's stuttering words, as though the two young men were in unison of thought and feeling:

> 'Knud Ulfson speaks to all the world!
> And this is what Knud Ulfson says:
> Neither the white bear of the wasteland,
> Nor the white ghost in the darkened hall;
> Neither blood, nor bone, flesh, nor entrails,
> Neither belly-wound nor eye-wound,
> Liver-wound nor arm-pit wound –
> Causes him fear, causes him delay
> In answering challenge!
> Knud Ulfson has outstared the breeding wolf;
> He has snatched the snake from its mossy shelter;
> He has held the bear's paw in his right hand.
> Knud Ulfson will not waver from Harald's blade,
> Will not avoid Harald's thrust,
> Will not shrink when Harald strikes;
> For though Harald is great,
> Knud Ulfson is greater;
> Though Harald kills Knud,
> They will go together to Valhalla!'

When Grummoch heard these words, even he shuddered, for he knew that now Knud had reached the outermost boundary of berserk madness, the point at which a viking's mind deserts him and he runs upon the spears gladly, laughing and joking, knowing not what he feels or says. Such men die without knowing they are dead; but always they take with them any who stand within reach of their blows. Such men make no effort to defend themselves, but set their heart only on delivering blows. . . .

Grummoch muttered from the corner of his spittle-flecked mouth, 'I stand beside you, Harald. When he comes in, I will strike his legs from under him with the shaft of my lance, then we will send him packing as he sprawls upon the ground!'

But Harald did not answer. His face was set and hard, like a face carved from wood. He slowly set himself, left foot forward, to meet the berserk's charge. His motions were deliberate. It was as though he stood before a king and prepared to make his bow. It was as though he stood before a lady and prepared to dance with her, in some high hall at the winter feasting. It was as though he was a statue carved in ivory; a statue of a man preparing to stand before death himself.

Then Knud Ulfson began to scream, high and in the rhythm of the little drum. Heome pounded the hollow gourd, beating out the pulses of the berserk's inner heart.

Then suddenly Heome himself twirled round thrice, shouted high in the barking of a dog, and ceased his drumming.

Knud Ulfson flung back his blood-stiffened plaits and charged, his lips drawn upwards so that his white teeth could be seen, clenched in a smile of death.

The red men on either side parted before him, their

axes now lowered, their eyes wide with wonder and fear.

Grummoch made to stand before Harald, but Sigurdson gave such a bull-like bellow that the giant fell to one side, his lance-point almost in the ground. And thus he learned that Harald Sigurdson wished to meet his fate alone, and with no aid from any man — not even from his dearest oath-brother, and the foster-father of his children, Svend and Jaroslav.

There are the moments in a man's life when he welcomes other folk about him, so that they may comfort him, bring him food, or presents, or the simple pleasure of kindly words. But there are other moments, which come but infrequently in a man's life, when he needs no other but himself to be beside him. These are the moments when food, and presents, and kindly words count as nothing; for the man stands before death himself, who is not concerned with food and presents and kindly words.

Before death, man stands alone, and no one may comfort him. Nor does he need comfort, for he is now aware that only he may pass through the low door into the darkness; that none may go with him, however much food, however many presents, however many kindly words they bear.

The man at the brink of death stands quite alone.

Harald Sigurdson stood quite alone that morning, upon the blood-slippery clay of the ancient burial mound, that had been there before the first red men carried their skin-wrapped packages across the frozen seas to the north. The hot sun beat down upon him, from a world outside man's knowledge; the hot sun burning down, thoughtlessly, upon another world of ants, some wearing feathers, some wearing iron helmets; ants, without sense in their movements, power in their minds; ants who must die one day, from sun, or frost, from hunger, or the letting out of blood; from the deep salt sea, where great creatures moved mindless among the weed. . . .

And as Harald Sigurdson stood, watching Knud Ulfson with eyes as keen as a hawk's, as through a crystal glass, sharp and clear – though the world of men about Knud was grey and misty and blind – Harald suddenly remembered poor Havlock Ingolfson, crying out as he drowned upon the lonely rocky skerry off the coast of Norway, with the bitter sea in his mouth, and the mocking sea birds screeching over him.

And when Knud was no more than a full lance-thrust away from him, Harald remembered the Shield-maiden, who had told him he had done wrong to leave the wretch, Havlock Ingolfson, to drown so miserably, he who had sailed the length and breadth of the world's seas in a cockleshell of a longship. She had said she would come twice, and now Harald felt that she was near, perhaps at the edge of the redstone quarry, or behind him, laughing, her white-golden hair in thick plaits, hanging to her waist, her broad shoulders held back, waiting for him to die and to go with her to Valhalla, where Thorfinn Thorfinnson waited with a new jest, and Gudbrod Gudbrodsson burnished his poor breastplate with an old piece of iron that he had found in a kitchen-midden in some village they had sacked in their earlier wicked days. . . .

Harald wished that Thorfinn and Gudbrod were there to see him now. He did not think of Asa, or his two young sons, Svend Sigurdson and Jaroslav Sigurdson. Nor did he think of poor Jamsgar Havvarson, who was a good fighter, but who had doubts about Thor and Odin, and wished sometimes that he had followed the Whitechrist.

Harald did not think of many things that morning, upon the slippery burial mound of the first stone-men, who painted their caves with pictures of bulls, and wore bones in their hair.

He did not hear the cry of the hawk and the carrion crow and the thunderbird above him. He did not hear Grummoch's weeping. He did not hear Knud Ulfson say suddenly, as he halted in his wild rush before his ship-master, the man who had taught him the usage of the axe, 'Harald Sigurdson, I am a fool who has come to his senses. I obey you in all things. I love you in all things. I am your man. Let us now fight as brothers!'

Harald did not hear these words. *For he too was a berserk.* . . .

His long-bladed Algonkin axe came down, precisely as a drawn line, without fear, without feeling; without mercy, or without hatred.

And Knud Ulfson died with a smile on his silly northern face, his plaits a yard apart from each other, his silly hands, smooth with no rowing, fingers wide, and weaponless.

For he had flung his weapons away at the foot of the hillock, when his grey-misted mind had cleared and had shown him Harald again as his true master.

And so, with a handful of men on either side left, the fight upon the burial mound ended, even as the thunderbird shrieked, calling a close to the dawn.

Those who had stood behind Heome and the dead berserk that morning now turned like whipped hounds and ran westwards, over the hot rock and the withered scrub, so that none of the tribes coming later to the great quarry should meet them and know that they had broken the peace which had always reigned over that sacred place. . . .

For all this had happened while other men were in their beds, and still dreaming of the day before them.

Chapter 24 *The Judgement of Gichita*

Old Gichita sat, towards midday, under a buffalo-hide awning, scratching the ears of his favourite dog, Weuk-weuk, and watching two young boys wrestling on the sandy soil before him, the rays of the sun glinting upon their copper-coloured backs as they strove to show their chieftain what warriors they would become.

The old braves and the grey-haired men of the Council stood or squatted behind Gichita, silently watching the contest, sometimes sipping from the water gourds at their sides, for the day was warm, though the chieftain had had his awning moved up onto the cliff-top, high above the great lake, so that he and his folk might enjoy what breeze there was. Far below them, the sheer cliff-face flattened out and dark trees grew down to the green water's edge. The longship lay at anchor, a bowshot out, her sail furled, her timbers dry and faded by the sun-light.

And as the boys wrestled and the old men nodded, waking only to whisk the flies away from them, a squaw suddenly stood up and wailed in a high and nasal tone, 'Aiee! Aiee! But ill-fortune comes, Gichita!'

The old man turned, angry with the woman for break-ing the warm silence. At first he could not see to what she was pointing, for there was a dust blowing across his sight, being old; and the heat of the day had drawn moisture out of the land to form a faint haze up there on the heights.

But at last he saw clearly the nature of the misfortune to which the woman referred. A handful of men were coming slowly along the shoulder of the hill. Gichita recalled that two score of men had gone forth that morning at dawn; but here were not more than six returning.

And as they came still closer, Gichita saw that of that six three only were red men, of his own folk, and the others were white strangers. His eyes picked out the giant Grummoch, who seemed to be half leading, half carrying Heome. Harald, the viking leader, was helping another white man to carry someone, who hung limp between them. The others walked slowly, like men who had come a long distance and were nigh exhausted.

Gichita called sharply for the two boys to stop wrestling. They did so, and crept, afraid, behind the awning. The old dog, Weuk-weuk, did the same, sensing that his master was troubled in his heart and wished not to be worried.

And then Gichita saw that the red man who was being carried by the two white ones was his own warrior son, Wawasha; and he knew from the way Wawasha's arm hung down that the brave was dead.

The squaws knew this also, and fell to their knees and covered their heads with dust. The older braves pulled their blankets over their eyes and shuffled away, so as not to be near Gichita when the greatest of his grief came upon him.

And so Harald and Grummoch returned, with dead Wawasha and gibbering Heome. And with them were only one other viking, and two sorely wounded Beothuk braves, besides Wawasha and Heome. The others lay stark in the sun upon the ancient burial mound, the birds already squabbling over them, the carrion-foxes sniffing about the base of the hill.

And Harald laid down the body of Wawasha before his father and, swaying with tiredness of mind and body, told the story of that bloody day above the sacred stone quarries.

And old Gichita listened, rocking backwards and forwards on his buffalo-hide pallet, moaning like a sick animal at his great loss. Now the drums of the women, the flat death-drums, began to murmur behind Harald's words, keeping up an undertone of grief in the sunlight.

And Harald said, 'Gichita, blood-father, our sadness is great, both yours and mine; for we have both lost a man we loved. Yet there is no profit in tears or in wailing, for they will not bring back laughter to dead lips, or sight to dead eyes. Wawasha is dead. The gods have taken him. There is no more to say.'

Harald stood for a while, leaning on his sword, *Peace-giver*, which he had taken up as they passed through the encampment on their way to the heights above the lake.

His face was drawn and haggard, filthy with blood and dust. His great arms were gashed, his clothing half cut from him. His hair hung damp and matted about his ears.

Grummoch sank to his knees now, his tawny head bowed with tiredness, his hands hanging before him as though they were asleep.

Heome stood between the two Beothuk braves, his thin lips twitching, the muscles of his pale face working as though they were ripples on the surface of a lake. His weak body was shaken from time to time with spasms, as though he were already an old man, ready for death.

And when the long silence had grown as heavy as a great weight of logs or of buffalo-meat, Gichita held up his hands for the squaws to begin their drumming again, for he was about to make his pronouncement, to speak his words of judgement, which a chief must speak.

At first his voice was flat and dead, like the sound of the night wind rustling among dry sedges; and then it gained more life, more fullness as he went on.

'Members of the Council, my braves, my white guests – blood has been shed. Tears will not bring it back. Vengeance will not bring it back. Nothing will ever bring it back. The warriors who have died, both red and white, will not come back and walk amongst us ever again, though we weep, though we cry for revenge. Wawasha will never sit by my side again. . . .'

The squaws began to wail at these words, and the old men of the Beothuk Council bowed their heads and murmured. Heome suddenly shook his wild head and began to beat upon the little drum that hung from his neck still, striking the skin with the heel of his hands, in unison with the other drums, as though he, too, mourned the dead.

Gichita stared at him as though he had never seen him before. And then he said, 'On whom should we call for revenge? Who is there worth the dead who lie on the hill for the wolves to carry away, now? There is only Heome; only Heome, who smiles and plays his little drum before you now, mourning his dead brother and all the braves who lie upon the hill. Those of you who have lost friends, or sons, have the blood right, if you choose to take it, the right to take vengeance on the man-thing who shudders before you. Those of you who wish may take the war-axe and let it speak to the head of Heome, poor Heome, who wished to be a brave but was denied by the gods. Take your vengeance now, old men; take it upon Heome, if that will satisfy you, if that will repay you for the strong sons you have lost.'

Harald looked up for a moment and saw the headman of the Council shaking his grizzled head, and heard him say, 'We of the Beothuk Council are beyond such acts of blood, Gichita. Though Heome died a score of times, that would not repay us for our lost sons.'

Harald saw the smile creep across the pale face of Heome, saw his great eyes suddenly blaze with a flat amber light, the look that comes into the eyes of a wolf when it slides safely away from its hunters and runs for freedom.

Harald gave a snort, to clear his nostrils of the foulness of the air, and, sick at heart with the memory of his dead friends, moved away from the group about the awning, to the edge of the tall cliff.

He saw the lake below, and the clustered pine-trees that bordered the lake. He saw *Long Snake* lolling on the waves, never more to be manned by Northmen, and then the tears began to run down his cheeks. As he stood there, with the breeze lifting his tangled bloody hair, he named his friends again, silently, as though in homage – Gudbrod Gudbrodsson, Thorfinn Thorfinnsson, Jamsgar Havvarson, Wawasha, and all the others.

For a fleeting instant, he even thought of the name of poor wretched Havlock Ingolfson who had screamed with the birds on the salt-caked skerry that night so long ago, deserted by Haakon Redeye, deserted by Harald Sigurdson, deserted even by Odin.... Only the Shield-maiden had spoken up for poor Havlock Ingolfson....

Then Harald heard Gichita say, 'My braves, you are generous. You will not kill my only son, Heome, and for that I, an old man, am grateful, for, poor thing that he is, he is all I have left now, the only blood I have.'

For an instant, Harald almost fell upon his knees before the old chief and offered to serve him as his son, all his life. But then he recalled Asa Thornsdaughter and his two sons, Svend and Jaroslav. . . . One day, one day, perhaps, he might get back to them again, beside the fjord. . . . One day, before the boys had grown to be men and had quite forgotten him. . . .

Then Heome spoke, and his voice was thin and trembling, like that of a bird, light and bodiless, fluttering above the heads of men, almost above their understanding.

'Heome, son of Gichita, brother to brave Wawasha, speaks to you. Listen and be silent, for Heome's voice is the voice of the gods, the voice of the raindrops, the voice of the little drum. In the pattering of my drum, hear ye now the voices of the rain, the torrents, the falling of leaves. Hear ye now the message that the first gods tried to bring to man but could not speak, for lack of tongues and hands. Heome lacks hands, too. He is like the gods, he is the gods! But Heome has a voice and a little drum, and the magic of the gods is in that drum. Hark!'

Then he gave such a blow on the taut skin that it split across, like a gaping mouth. But Heome did not notice that, and went on beating at the soundless gourd, his stiff hands moving in a frenzy.

'Hark ye! Hark ye!' he intoned now. 'In the thunder of my drum speaks the voice of the great mountains, the enormous forests. Out of my drum comes the call of the Wendigo, the horned beast that quests for the bodies and souls of men through the snow wastes and down along the lakesides. Those of you who would live, listen to that voice, for I am the Wendigo, the questing beast, the . . .'

Then Gichita, the old chief, drew his withered hand across his eyes, and groaned with anguish. To the brave who stood beside him, he said in a broken voice, 'Take the poor fool and bind his hands and feet. The gods have stolen his senses away and they will not return. Heome has killed his brother and now his heart will never be whole. From now on he shall live with the squaws and the young children, for he is no fit companion of men. It had been better to have killed him, my braves, in vengeance.'

Harald heard these words, suffering that the old man should have been caused to speak them. Then suddenly he heard other words, which he did not understand, until it was too late. They were the words of crazed Heome.

'Viking dog,' he screamed, 'on *your* shoulders lies the blame! Until you came, we were a folk of peace!'

Then suddenly Heome was running forward with a slithering, scurrying rush, the red dust rising about his legs, his shrivelled hands whirling like those of a scarecrow. And he was upon Harald before the viking knew it, before he could prepare.

Then Harald heard the high cry of alarm from the braves under the buffalo-skin awning, and saw Grummoch rise and put his great hands before his staring eyes.

And then, cackling like a night-hawk, Heome flung his arms about Harald and toppled him to the crumbling edge of the cliff above the great lake.

The two fell from sight, one screaming, one silent.

When the giant Grummoch reached the cliff edge, all he saw was a rivulet of stones that raced madly down in a shroud of red dust.

Grummoch and the one remaining viking made their way down the slope towards the lake, followed by those of the braves who could still perform such feats.

The viking, a small man called Thorgeif, from Lakkesfjord, no great hand with axe, but a fine sailor, said, 'If Harald's fall was broken by a bed of moss, such as grows down here in the dampness, he might yet be alive.'

Grummoch did not answer, so great was his grief.

Thorgeif said again, 'Or if he fell into the boughs of a tree, they would save his life, perhaps.'

Then Grummoch turned upon the man and swore at him, harshly, not meaning to hurt him, but too full of grief to hold his tongue. Then Thorgeif was silent, and ran with the sweat coursing down his face and his thin jaws set.

And at last they found Harald Sigurdson, not on a bed of moss, or in the boughs of a tree, but on the toothed edge of a rock-shoulder, lying like a broken doll, but still breathing.

At his feet lay Heome, smiling but dead, the broken drum still about his neck, and the sword *Peace-giver* through him.

Thorgeif said in his simple way, 'Harald must have rammed this message home even as they fell. There was never such a fighter before.'

Then Harald, from the rock from which Grummoch

dared not try to move him, said in a whisper, 'I have struck many shrewd blows, Thorgeif Rammson of Lakkesfjord, where the flax grows better than anywhere else in the Northland, but this was my masterpiece. It had to be done swiftly, or the wolf might have gone scot free to trouble others.'

Grummoch laved Harald's head with water from the lake.

'Lie easy, brother,' he said, 'and do not talk.'

Harald smiled and nodded gently. But in a short while he whispered again, 'That was a good blow, was it not, Grummoch? Did you ever see a better blow? And all done in the air! Where is Thorfinn? He should make a song about it. Where is Thorfinn?'

While Thorgeif knelt down and began to weep, Grummoch told Harald that Thorfinn was in the woods, looking for a hare for dinner, though the words almost choked him to speak.

Harald said, smiling, 'He was always a great fellow for his stomach, that Thorfinn . . . I remember, out on the seal-skerries beyond Isafjord, one autumn . . . I remember . . . I remember . . .'

But Harald Sigurdson did not say what he remembered, for those things suddenly seemed to be of little importance to him.

Then, with the grave-faced red men about him, he whispered again at last, 'Asa Thornsdaughter, and my two sons, Svend and Jaroslav, are waiting above the fjord to see Long Snake come in to haven, Grummoch. I have just seen them, and they send their dear love, my friend.'

Now the giant Grummoch turned away his tangled tawny head and let the salt tears run as they pleased. He heard Harald say, 'On the way home, let us pick up poor Havlock Ingolfson from the skerry. He will be mighty cold, Grummoch . . . mighty cold now, after a winter in the icy seas.'

Old Gichita was carried on his litter to Harald's side, and touched the viking, with fingers as gentle as those of a woman, upon the ruined forehead.

'Go easy, my son,' he said, 'you have nothing to fear. You are a man. The gods know that and wait for you.'

And though he spoke in the red men's tongue, Harald heard him and understood him and opened his eyes for the last time and said, 'Red Father, I go easy and my hand is in the hand of my brother, Wawasha. He stands beside me now, smiling that we are together again.'

Then Harald gave a little shiver and shook his head a time or two. At that moment, a skein of geese flew over the pine woods, the air whistling in their pinions.

Harald's voice came from far away and his eyes were closed now.

'The Shield-maiden has come with her swans,' he said. 'Do you not hear them?'

Grummoch bent over him and clasped his cold hand. Then all the braves bowed down their feathered heads as they passed the rock on which the viking lay, in their last homage.

And at last, when it seemed that the world had stopped in its courses through the sky, Gichita lifted up his head and wiped his eyes.

'The three of them shall go together,' he said. 'At last Heome shall be with warriors.'

And so *Long Snake* was brought to shore by the braves, and her deck piled high with the resinous wood of the fir tree; and Harald was laid with his sword, *Peace-giver*, in his right hand, and with Wawasha on the one side of him and Heome on the other.

In Wawasha's hand the red men placed a war-axe; but Heome's hands were still stiff and useless, even now, and they were forced to lay his axe upon his chest, beside the broken war-drum.

As the sun was sinking below the far hills, the red men flung tarry torches among the dried wood, and then set *Long Snake* off on her voyage, with the wind of evening in her parched sail.

She was twenty bowshots away when the red flames leaped the length of her mast and ate up the wood and the hide of the sail; she was thirty bowshots away when the flames ravened down to her waterline.

And then, still flaring like a great furnace, *Long Snake* slipped below the surface of the lake, just as the distant sun fell from sight behind the hills.

Thorgeif said softly to Grummoch, 'I have sailed with Harald Sigurdson since he was a lad – by North Sea, White Sea and Middle Sea. But I never thought to see him sail away and leave me in a strange land, among foreign men.'

Grummoch turned from the lake and put his great arm about Thorgeif's shoulders.

'We shall have each other to speak Norse to in the evening time,' he said slowly. 'A man must be thankful even for small mercies in this world.'

Then, to cover their grief, they walked together, chanting an old feast-hall ditty from Jomsburg, about a man who put his arm round a bear in the darkness, thinking it was his sweetheart.

But before they reached the bright fires of the Beothuk encampment, they were silent again. For a while there would be nothing worth saying. They knew that well enough.